A SE̶N̶ ̶ ̶ ̶ ̶ ̶ ̶L̶E̶
and other stories

In this thought-provoking and sensitive collection of short stories, young people find themselves up against prejudice, hypocrisy and bewilderment. There's Lorraine and Mohammed who fall wildly in love, ever conscious of the family pressures which might force them apart; John feels trapped by his marriage and the birth of his son, neither of which he is emotionally ready for; Jim finds himself on trial for a violent crime after he accidentally becomes caught up in a demonstration, and Tony, who despises the mindless prejudice of this school-mates, is himself dealt a nasty blow by the people he seeks to defend.

Jan Needle observes with great compassion and sometimes humour the passion, despair and hopes of young people growing up in the urban life of the 1980s.

Other titles by Jan Needle
in Fontana Lions

GOING OUT
MY MATE SHOFIQ
THE SIZE SPIES
ANOTHER FINE MESS
ALBESON AND THE GERMANS

Jan Needle

A SENSE OF
SHAME

and other stories

FONTANA · LIONS

First published in Great Britain 1980
by André Deutsch Ltd
First published in Fontana Lions 1982
by William Collins Sons & Co Ltd
8 Grafton Street, London WIX 3LA
Third Impression January 1984

© 1980 by Jan Needle

Printed in Great Britain by
William Collins Sons & Co. Ltd, Glasgow

For Terry and Pat

Contents

White Man's Burden

TONY ROBERTSON walked down the Ashton Road as if his feet had springs on them. It was a cold and crispy night, with the strings of orange road lights climbing over the moors sparkling as he looked at them. The stars were sparkling, too, just like they were meant to, and he giggled. 'Twinkle twinkle little star,' he sang. Or mumbled. Half sang – half mumbled. He was a bit piddled.

He stopped for a moment and threw his head back, taking in great snuffs of the cold, biting air. There wasn't a lot of wind, even off the moors, so he wasn't cold in himself. But the air roaring into his lungs was like ice. It made him feel dizzy. Elated and dizzy. He was really chuffed. As his eyes blurred and cleared with the deep breathing and look-ing straight up, he caught a sight of Orion, the only star constellation he knew the name of, except the Great Bear, which everyone knew. I like Orion, he thought muzzily. Great. The Giant-Hunter and his dog. He giggled again. Pretty daft name for a dog, though – Sirius. 'Here, boy,' he shouted, under his breath. 'Come on, boy, come on, Sirius. Eat up your Pedigree Chum. Full of giant-bone jelly!'

He looked behind him, back over the big roundabout on the by-pass, back towards the Cat's Pyjamas. It had been a belting night, really smashing. The group had been fantas-tic, and until the rum and black had got too far into his brain for him to concentrate any more, he'd been picking up some great tips watching the bass guitarist. He was a black bloke, from Moss Side, and he was great. Tony ran his fingers up and down an imaginary guitar, leaning against a lamp-post. He waved as some people in a passing car stared at him. Peasants. It was his birthday in three weeks, he'd be sixteen. And the new amplifier was in the bag, no danger. The old man had virtually promised it. Nice to have a father who had plenty of loot. They'd got the new carpets and the decorating done, Sally had left college and wasn't costing them any more, and Sam had decided to go to the comprehensive, so that'd save on fees. Little thicko, be a waste of time him going to grammar anyway. Loot, loot, loot. With the new amp they'd be able to look out for gigs. Real ones. Make their own money. And he could give up running the disco in Manchester. That was a drag if ever there was one.

Tony shivered suddenly. Time to get moving again. He'd read somewhere that alcohol cooled your blood, which was why tramps often died in cells. They chucked 'em in full up to here of meths, with one rotten tatty blanket in case they spewed all over it, and then a couple of hours later they'd find 'em dead. Blood temperature dropped through the alcohol, no proper clothes, one crummy blanket. And . . . He made a noise to signify death. And shivered again. Even through his new black leather trench coat that he'd had for Christmas he shivered. Brass monkeys.

As he pushed himself off from the lamp-post and steered unsteadily down the Ashton Road, it occurred to Tony that it was probably deliberate. About the tramps. The police weren't stupid, even if they were pigs. They probably knew damn well it would kill the tramps, chucking them in cold cells. It was probably a policy. He giggled briefly as it struck him they probably got bounty money, like for killing squirrels. Five pounds a tail. But he stopped laughing. Swine, he thought, angrily. Evil swine! It probably was true. They probably did get a fiver.

His old man hated him going on about the pigs, and they had rows about it sometimes. But his old man was getting past it these days. He'd been a socialist once, a union man. Now he was too well-off to know. He'd lost his fire. He didn't give a damn. Every time they talked about something happening in the paper, even a strike by some poor starving hospital workers or something, he took the wrong side. It made Tony see red, get absolutely fuming. And he never got used to it. He could remember so clearly when it had been different. Not so long ago, neither. He'd brought Tony up to be a liberal, to reckon on everybody being equal, having the same rights and so on. Then he'd turned. He'd changed. Now he ranted on like something out of the *Daily Telegraph*. Crazy.

Over to his left, from the Ashton Road towards the edge of the snowy moors, was Rose Bank, where the blacks and Pakistanis lived. Despite himself, Tony felt his legs begin to go a bit quicker. He snorted, annoyed, and forced himself to slow down. He pressed the button on his digital watch, then waited, swaying, till his eyes slowly focused. Ten to twelve. He snorted again. That was it, see, he was catching it from his old man. He was actually afraid of being dragged off and beaten up or something. He laughed. But it was serious. That's what his old man truly believed. Crazy. And sad.

Tony felt a rush of meaningless affection. It was a strange, warm, drunken sensation, as though he was going to burst into tears. In fact his eyes did get wet. He had to blink, then rub the back of his hand over them. He stopped, confused, feeling the warmth flooding through him, then looked with affection at the dark, cramped terraces of Rose Bank. He loved them, the people who lived down there. Really. He was glad they were here, in England. He loved blacks. All of them. West Indians, Pakistanis, Bengalis (he knew the difference, he found himself thinking proudly). There was a daft smile of self-satisfaction on his face. He loved them. But what had gone wrong, with Dad? He'd been for them once, Tony could recall it well. Defended them against all-comers. Then it had changed.

In front of him, as he slowly wandered along, Tony saw some people. He rubbed his wet eyes once more. They were a long way off, and he couldn't tell how many of them there were, or what age, or what colour. He felt vaguely worried, disturbed. It was nearly midnight, and this wasn't the safest place in the world to be wandering along on his Tod. He laughed nervously. Didn't matter about colour, that wasn't the point. You could get robbed and kicked up by a white gang just as easy as a black. His mouth was dry, so he swallowed. A vision of the Cat's Pyjamas swum into his head. Gee, he could use another rum and black, no danger.

His mouth had a sweetish taste, from the blackcurrant, and he wished he smoked, because a fag would probably cure it. He stared some more. They were a long way off still, but maybe he should cross over. It was a dual carriageway, with a wide central reservation, and the other side was altogether a posher sort of deal. Old folks flats, big streets leading up the hill towards the grammar school. He glanced up and down. Not a lot of traffic. Perhaps he would go across. Safer. And he had to cross somewhere, anyway, to get along to Miller Road and home.

The feeling of affection that had surprised him a few moments before turned quickly into a feeling of self-disgust. He stood leaning against a rail cursing himself. That's just about ruddy typical, he thought, that's just about it with you, Robertson! Your old man would be proud of you. There you are, thinking how they're real people, just like anyone else, as much right to be here as you have, then you see some in front of you and you nearly wet yourself. You slob. You gutless slob. Ten years time and you'll be just like him. Send 'em home! Lock 'em up! Whip the devils! You make me feel sick. He bit his lip and remembered some of the rows they'd had recently. The ructions when he'd pointed out that the great and glorious Enoch himself was the Health Minister who had asked the Commonwealth brothers to come, to get the Health Service out of the mire. My God, that had been a good one. You'd have thought he'd found Mum in bed with the coalman. He'd been accused of lying, straightforward lying. Just for telling the truth! His mother had actually told him off over that row. Not because she'd taken sides, she just hated them to fight. She'd said the old man was not himself. Lot of strain at the office. All that garbage. One good point though, although she'd said it like half a joke: if he has a heart attack, my laddo, bang goes your new amp. Rock on, Mother! They'd had a laugh over that.

When he'd brought Mustafa home that time, it had been different, of course. You couldn't be rude, could you? His old man had sat at the tea table like a great fool, completely tongue-tied. Mum had been dead embarrassed, with not knowing if he ate English food or drank proper tea. Thought he might want it with no sugar and a lump of lemon, as if he was a rotten Russian! Tony had enjoyed himself for a while, till the novelty wore off. But it hadn't been so easy after, up in his room. Mustafa wasn't really into the same sort of music, and he wasn't interested in Tony's guitar or the group or anything. And when Tony had finally suggested they nip down the Waggon for a pint or a rum he'd looked right shocked. For a start-off, he didn't drink. He'd tried quite hard to get mates with Mustafa, but nothing'd come of it. He was the only Pakistani in his year, at the grammar school, so he must've needed a pal, someone to go about with. But he didn't seem that bothered, when it got down to it. Leastways he never tried to seek Tony out, at school. And there wasn't a return invite. Pity, that. He must've needed a pal.

With a start Tony realised that he hadn't crossed over, was just wandering along head down, thinking. When he came out of his dream he could hear voices, quite clear. He looked up, a swoop of fear gripping his stomach. They were

13

about a hundred yards away, a big gang, six or eight of them. He gulped. They were white, all right, he could see their faces in the street lamps, and hear their English voices. Despite the cold, the dribs and drabs of snow in the gutters, they didn't seem to have coats on. Bomber jackets, leather some of them, by the look of the gleams. Leather. Tony's mouth went dry. Damn fool, he'd make a great ruddy target, no danger. Standing there in his full-length leather gear and his thirty quid boots. He had rich kid written all over him. He kept on walking, but it was more a creep now. He was doing about half a mile an hour. They were looking at him. They'd stopped talking. They were sizing him up. The clouds of breath in front of Tony, twin streams from his nostrils, were getting quicker. He could feel his heart beginning to thump. You ruddy fool, he thought. You're just asking for it.

There wasn't a lot of point in making a run for it, and even less trying to flag down a car. No one in their right mind would stop if they saw a gang of thugs belting up a bloke. He wouldn't stop himself, he knew. Not much of a world for Good Samaritans, these days, even if it ever had been. Come to think of it, though, the Good Samaritan came afterwards. No one stopped when the guy was actually getting the battering. He sized up the road again. If he nipped across now he could get into the car park by the Mare and Foal, then across the waste land. He shuddered. Not likely, though. Much better to get done over on the main road, much better. You never knew your luck: the pigs might come along in a prowl-car and save your life!

It was now or never, for sure. And it was never. When the gang were fifty yards away he heard a familiar voice call: 'Wotcher, Robertson. You're out late on your own, aren't you?'

The sense of relief was almost comic. Tony felt utterly silly, his knees went all like jelly. The alcohol rushed to his head, making him feel giddy and sick. An idiot grin almost split his face. As he called back his voice squeaked, and he had to start again. There were a few nasty laughs from the gang.

'Hiya, Stephens,' he got out at last. 'Whereya been? I been down the Cat's Pyjamas. Bit sloshed. Been drinking rum and black.'

The gang slowly came up to him and stood there, under a light, their breaths rising into a cloud. Some of it was smoke, and again Tony felt the need for a fag. He was shaking slightly, aware that he'd just got away with murder – his murder! Stephens and three of the other lads were in his class. They were the school roughs, the ones that the headmaster was always ticking about in assembly, the ones he reckoned gave the grammar school a bad name – like a comprehensive, for instance. But Tony knew he was safe, so he didn't care. They wouldn't thump him at any rate. No quarrel. The other four lads he didn't know, but they all looked the same. Jeans, bomber jackets. They must be freezing, he thought. Playing hardmen.

'We been looking for some Pakis,' said Stephens. He said it provocatively, because he knew all about Tony's views. 'Some of your dirty little mates. To smash up.'

Tony said nothing. He gave a smile, pretending to be indifferent. He shrugged.

'You look petrified,' said Stephens. 'Hey, I bet you thought *we* was Pakis, didn't you? You're all shaking, lad. I bet you thought we was a gang, didn't you?'

'Comin' to duff you up,' said one of the others. He took the last drag on a cigarette and flicked the butt at a passing car.

Tony licked the inside of his mouth to try and get it wet.

'Nah,' he said. 'Too drunk to care. I've been down the Cat's Pyjamas.' His lips made a smacking noise, from dryness.

'Down the Cat's Pyjamas,' mimicked Stephens. 'Ooh, you dirty beast! Front or back?'

15

Everyone laughed, including Tony. He tried to think of a joke reply, but he couldn't. He didn't like this lot, he feared and despised them. Bullies. Thugs and bullies. They could smack him up and he had to be polite. Pretending to be friends.

'We been down Rose Bank,' said Stephens. 'Get ourselves a few black scalps. Give 'em a taste of the silent majority. Welcome to our land, brothers. Have a brick through the windowpane. Made in England! Pigs.'

'Yeah,' said Tony. 'Ah well, Stephens. I better be going. I've ... I've got some homework to finish.'

He heard someone say 'Ponce' about him, in the gang, quite loud. He pretended not to notice.

'Homework,' said Stephens. 'We've given the Pakis some, too. Putting in new glass. Much more fun.' He looked closely at Tony, a sort of leer on his face. 'Why don't you come out with us one night, eh Tone? Come out and bash up a few black brethren, eh? You look real good in that long coat. Like something out of the war. You know; Gestapo. Geheimnis Staats Polizei. Ge. Sta. Po. Thank gawd for a grammar school education!'

They all fell about. Tony felt mocked, insulted. He kept his mouth shut.

'Oh, but I forgot,' Stephens went on. 'You love 'em, don't you, Tone? Tony Robertson, the black man's friend. You're a bit of a pillock on the sly, aren't you, Tony?'

Before Tony had to reply, one of the others gave a hiss. They all turned, sharply, under the yellow street light. Not twenty yards away, walking steadily towards them, were two Pakistanis.

'Ee, ruddy hell,' said Stephens, quietly. 'Look at that pair of clowns. They must be mad.'

The two Pakistanis were not talking, and not pretending to look away. One of them was old, in his mid-thirties, and the other one much younger, almost a youth. Probably twenty-one or two. They both had on the mock-suede jackets with furry collars that you saw so many of on Pakistani mill workers that they were practically like a uniform. Under the short coats they had on thin brown cotton trousers and lightweight, plasticky shoes. They looked cold, frozen, and they had their hands deep in their pockets.

Tony felt sick, but also interested. The two weren't going to cross the road or anything, they were going to go straight past. He didn't know what the hell would happen. He didn't know if Stephens and his gang really chucked bricks through windows or whether they were just mouth. He didn't have the faintest idea if these two Pakistanis would be beaten up or if it was just bravado, kids' stuff. But as they approached, the tension in the air became amazing. The columns of breath, he noticed, had become intense, erratic, the sound of breathing sharper, very audible. And his own breathing – had stopped! He became aware of bursting lungs. He tried to let the air out smoothly, quietly, but it juddered, hissed, then whooshed out in a rush. Then he dragged in a huge gulp and held his breath once more.

As the two men got very close there was an outbreak of nervous conversation in the gang. It was whispered, mean-ingless, as though they were trying to pretend that nothing was happening, that they were just a bunch of lads standing under a streetlight on a perfectly normal midnight. The tension truly was electric. Every muscle in Tony's body was keyed up like a violin string. His arms ached with muscular strain.

'Hey, Stephens,' he said suddenly. It was an attempt to break the strain, to burst the tension, but it came out as a croak. He swallowed.

And then they were there. And there was an almost hysterical babbling, not loud, still almost whispers. As the Pakistanis walked past, carefully not brushing the white boys on the wide, snowy pavement, there was this babble of quiet noise. The tension in the air suddenly went upwards, increased, like an almost visible column, as though the boys' hatred of their own cowardice had built up like a head of steam and exploded into the air.

'You black bastards. You black bastards. You black bastards!' Stephens was gritting the words through his teeth, grinding them out in a sort of rage as he searched around for something to throw. But there was nothing, and it was not loud enough, hardly loud enough to hear. It wasn't until the Pakistanis were yards away that the gang began to shout. Then suddenly they'd turned a corner, down a road into Rose Bank. Out of earshot. Past caring.

Tony spat, because his mouth was like a dustman's glove. He felt no elation at the gang's cowardice. He started off across the road without looking at them. Time to go home, time to go home; God that rum, he must've been mad.

When he was on the central reservation, walking along in the same direction as the Pakistanis had gone, before crossing behind some cars that were coming along, he heard Stephens shout: 'Next time we'll show 'em, Robertson. When there's no ruddy grasser like you to drop us in it. We've done enough for tonight, but next time they won't stand a chance. You slimy little teacher's pet.'

He ignored them, and crossed behind the cars. He walked along, still unsteady, towards the Mare and Foal. After a bit he began to giggle. What a bunch of creeps! The gutless little creeps! Chucking bricks! Beating up Pakistanis! They couldn't knock the skin off a macaroni pudding! He saw the brown men in his mind's eye, walking steadily towards the boys. A whole gang, eight of them, nine including him. And they walked straight past, never a sideways glance. That just showed who the cowards were, eh? That just ruddywell showed. He got another mental picture then, of telling his Dad. His Dad reckoned that Asians were gutless. Not fighters like the British. No use talking to *him* about the Ghurkas! But this would be a laugh. He couldn't wait to tell him.

As he set off up the side of the Mare and Foal car park he looked back across the Ashton Road. The gang were almost out of sight, straggling along towards the town centre. Strangely, the two Pakistanis had come back out of the side street and were looking down the main road after them. He assumed it was the same pair, anyway, although it was hard to be sure in the dark. Bound to be, having a look at the gang who'd reckoned to terrify 'em. The warm feeling of love came back to Tony's stomach. They were terrific.

He was almost across the waste ground past the car park when he heard the noise. It was a clank, like someone stepping on a piece of corrugated iron. His stomach gave a leap and he looked back across the snow-whitened croft. There were two men close behind him, only ten or twelve yards. The Pakistanis.

Tony stopped, uncertain. They did not. Without a word they covered the thirty feet of rough ground and began to beat him up, silently, without even grunting. He stood upright for the first few punches, stunned, completely stunned, by the injustice of it. Once, he opened his mouth to say something, to point out, politely and with reason, that they'd got the wrong man. But a fist slammed into his open mouth, and his lip split, and his mouth filled with salty blood. Even when he lay on the ground, in the snow, feeling their cheap, pathetic shoes kicking his stomach, sides and head, he was more *hurt*, mentally hurt, than in pain. He couldn't believe it, he just couldn't believe it was happening.

It wasn't a severe beating-up, as beatings-up go. After a while they stood above Tony, panting. He lay on his back looking at the spinning stars, feeling the blood running down his throat, and thinking for no very clear reason: 'So. Pakistanis put the boot in, too. Dad will enjoy that bit, anyway.' He didn't feel quite real.

19

The older man, panting like a dog, said something in a language that Tony recognised – with a twinge of pride – as Urdu. The younger man replied, quietly, and they turned to go.

Then, immediately, in a huge rush, Tony felt desolate. Miserable. And incredibly, horribly hurt. He couldn't let them go, he couldn't. Not without . . .

'What did you do *that* for?' he asked tearfully. 'What did you do *that* for?' He felt just like a little child, a baby, who's been unfairly punished.

They looked down at him, panting clouds of breath against the glittering stars. The young man spoke, his accent very thick. He looked serious, as though the question needed a reply.

'You say black bastard,' he said. 'Bad thing. You call us black bastard.'

Tears rolled out of Tony's eyes down into his ears. He turned his head on one side to hide them, but he sobbed despite himself. He pulled up his fist and put his forefinger in his mouth, and bit it, hard.

'It's not *fair*,' he said, snorting and snuffling. 'It's just not *fair*. It wasn't . . . it wasn't . . . it wasn't . . . Oh it's not *fair*.'

With an effort, he turned his head back towards the stars. With an effort, he opened his eyes. He *had* to explain. It wasn't him. He liked them. He *loved* them.

Orion was looking down at him, without a lot of interest. Orion and his dog. But there was no one else. They'd gone.

Prejudice Rules OK!

IT WAS ALL a bit of a hoot really, looking back on it. But even I had to admit that as a holiday it was a total disaster. The only good thing that came out of it is it opened up my father's eyes to something or other – although I'm not quite sure what. I tell you this, though – he was never the same afterwards about the Welsh. Which considering his job is the biggest laugh of all. He's a lecturer, see – a senior lecturer to give him his full bit – in Race Studies, among other things. At a university. Which *has* tended to mean, over the years, that we've got a tiny amount brassed off with hearing him go on about brotherly love, and all equal under the skin and such-like garbage I mean true or not hardly matters to us – me and my sister Julie, that is – we don't give a monkey's. Just get fed up to the back teeth with hearing the old fellow drone on and on.

Well anyway, the fun began to start when we got deep into the heart of Welshest Wales. We'd come from up north of Manchester way, and we'd been driving for hours. The old man's quite good company – better in a way since Mum left, because he seems a lot more relaxed – and being as how he's pretty well off we've got this dirty great German car – a BMW, dead fast and that. So we'd been on the road a good long while before it got boring. But when we'd sung all the songs we *all* knew (i.e. three, that we learned at our mother's knee and other low joints) for the ninety-ninth time, and talked about how nice it was of Professor Green to lend us the cottage and that, the conversation was getting rather thin round the edges. When Dad started warbling 'Riding Down to Bangor on the Eastern Train' yet again, Julie called a halt.

'Come on, Daddy,' she said – she's got this rather posh voice, has Julie, although she's a right little raver on the quiet, I reckon. 'I know – we *all* know – we're going towards Bangor, but not again. Silence is golden, eh? How about it?'

The old fellow got a trifle miffed by this. Julie's nearly seventeen, and as I said, I don't think there's a lot of virginity left in her, but he still tends to see her as his little girl. I could see that he'd probably go all haughty and bring up manners and so on, so I looked round for something to comment on.

And bang off I saw it. Up front about three hundred yards was a big signpost. It was in English all right – we were, after all, in the United Kingdom – but you could hardly tell that at all. It had been vandalised. Done over. All the English names were gone completely. And painted over the top were all these daft Welsh words – you know the type, all gees, doubleyous and ells.

'Hey, look at that, Dad,' says I, all innocent. 'What have they done that for? I can't tell if we're riding down to Bangor or not.' (It's quite useful still being only just fifteen – you can play the kid with the best of them.)

He took his foot off the gas for a while till we'd studied the signpost.

'Defaced,' he said. (Gee, thanks for the info, Dad!) 'Stupid oafs. It's a good job we know where we're heading for.'

Julie, who was obviously bored out of her mind and ready for anything, saw a golden opportunity for a laugh.

'Defaced?' she said, in a mock amazed voice. 'Really, Daddy! That coming from you! It *is* their country, you know.'

I glanced at the old fellow's face in the driving mirror. He

22

was trying to make up his mind whether to take the bait. I helped him along.

'Yeah, be fair, Dad. I mean, they probably get right fed up being pushed around by the Brits. Why shouldn't they have road signs in their own language?'

He was hooked. He went on at great length about how it was only a minority of them, how it would harm their economic development, how vandalism and violence never got anybody anywhere (not much!). You know the sort of stuff; I won't bore you by trotting it out again. Julie played him like a fish – she's very good at it. Because she knew, anyway, that there'd been some talk with Professor Green about the problem of the holiday cottage: you know, the Welsh resented houses being left empty most of the year, and holiday homes pushing up cottage prices till the locals couldn't afford to live there, and that. They even burned down the odd isolated one every now and then to make their point! She finally said, very sweetly: 'I'm not sure that we're in a particularly good moral position to judge, Daddy. I mean, three well-off English people coming to spend a week in a cottage owned by another foreigner who hardly ever visits. If I were a Welsh person I think I might object very strongly.'

The old fellow was incensed.

'Look,' he ranted, 'this is just ridiculous. Of course one is against holiday homes in general, if they damage the local economy, but in North Wales that just *does not* apply. Good Lord, girl, the whole economy here is *based* on tourism. And mainly English tourism, at that. If it weren't for people like us these people would be poor, desperately poor. They might even have had to move out to live.'

'Golly,' said Julie, quick as a flash. 'Not *more* immigrants into England? That would be terrible.'

'Puffballs,' says I, anxious to dig the knife in while I'd got the chance. 'If they were immigrants the old fellow would love them, wouldn't you, Dad?'

23

He drove along in silence for a few minutes, regaining his cool, like. Then he laughed, still on the shortish side, though.

'Daft kids,' he said. 'You'll see when we get there. Most people in Wales are absolutely opposed to this sort of nonsense. Completely. And they recognise – all sensible people recognise – that these Welsh language freaks do an enormous amount of harm, and practically no good at all. They're damaging their own case. *And* the language, I shouldn't wonder. Most Welsh people don't speak it. Imagine how *they* must feel, having it forced down their throats.'

'But I thought Professor Green was very worried—' Julie began. She was turned off.

'Enough, Julie, enough. The locals in the village will be as nice as pie, as friendly as anything, you'll see. And I'll eat my hat . . . well, I'll be very surprised indeed if we find much Welsh spoken. It's the same as in England. Too much can be made of the race thing, you know. We'll have a splendid time.'

All right; conversation closed. I sat back and looked at the view, which even I had to admit – and I need views like I need a hole in the head – was pretty fantastic. The road was winding past Mount Snowdon (you could see why it was called that from the snow on top! Sorry.) and past a series of big, empty, black, freezing-looking lakes. Not much farther on we took a side road – complete with defaced signpost – and started going down into a valley. It was amazing, honest. Frightening windy roads, with a huge drop on one side and cliffs on the other completely blotting out the sun. Thank God for the BMW. It stuck to the road like muck to a muffin. But we all felt rather nervous when we arrived in the village.

Ten minutes later we were a hell of a lot more nervous, I can tell you. In fact, the old fellow had almost done himself a brain-damage with rage. Because the Welsh-

24

language freaks had had a go at much more than just the signposts!

It wasn't hard to find the cottage. Professor Green had said there was just the one pub – it had a Welsh name, so I can't tell you what it was – and the cottage was on the end of a terrace in a sort of little village square just behind it. He'd said it was the village meeting place, where people gathered for a chat, and it wasn't difficult to see why. Rather than being a square it was actually a triangle, with good low walls to sit on, a view down to a big lake, and the pub as handy as it could be. When we drew up outside the terrace, the square was empty, which was rather strange. But we guessed why in two minutes flat.

The only empty cottage was on the end of the terrace, right enough – any fool could see that. But it appeared to be derelict. The front door was hanging half open, with a stream of garbage strewn over the step, and three or four of the window panes were smashed. We sat in the car puzzled for a minute or two, listening to the silence after the engine was turned off. It *was* silent, too. Eerie. Then Julie jumped out, looked in the open front door of the ruin, and came back. Her face was white.

'The rotten pigs,' she said. 'They've done it over. It's all smashed up.'

Like I said, the old dad went hairless when he looked. He was all for thundering down the road and calling in the Polizei – much good that would have done him, being as how they were Welsh, an' all. But before he blew up completely, a little white-haired lady came trogging up from the other end of the terrace. She knocked on the front door and came in, and she had a broom and a big cardboard box in her mitts. Dad looked as if he might throttle her, but she just glanced around and said: 'You'll be needing a hand, I reckon. I'm Mrs Roberts from Number Three. Bit of a mess, isn't it.'

We were speechless. She could say that again! All the

cutlery was over the floor, the curtains were torn, the table and chairs were upsidedown. Julie was still white, as white as a sheet. And Dad was trembling with fury. A bit of a mess.

Mrs Roberts didn't explain, or apologise or anything. She only spoke a few words in fact, and then said Sorry, but she didn't speak English so good – she'd got out of the habit. (Pity the old fellow had decided not to put his hat in the bet after all.) So after a while we sort of fell into a routine of helping her – there didn't seem much else to do. In a surprisingly short time the place was straight enough to live in – we were on holiday, so you expect it to be a trifle rough, don't you? The only things we couldn't do anything about were the smashed windows and the daubed walls. The daubs were upstairs, and quite intriguing, in a way. Lots and lots of slogans – more doubleyous and double-ells than soft Mick – but all in Welsh. Rather decorative, but not very informative, if you know what I mean. Then, at the bottom, above one of the bed-heads, was written in bright red, in English: Keep Wales Welsh. Mrs Roberts disappeared and came back with some cardboard, which she stuck up in the windows, then said Sorry, but she didn't have enough food in to invite us. Julie said it was all right, we had sandwiches, and she trogged off, quiet as a mouse.

The old fellow stood in the middle of the downstairs floor – there was only a front room and a back kitchen – and scratched his head. Then he looked at his watch.

'Well, kids,' he said. 'It's too late to go back. Put a proper jacket on, John, to make yourself look a bit older. You'll do as you are, Julie. And if anyone asks you, you can't speak the language, right, but you're eighteen. We're going for a pint.'

I could have kissed the old fellow, honest I could. I like a pint myself – but I never thought I'd hear him offer me one – and Julie drinks like a fish. So we slammed and locked the front door and set out across the triangular square jollier than we'd have thought possible an hour or so before. It was darkish by this time, and the village meeting place had filled up. Mostly teenagers, and distinctly unfriendly. The way they looked at you was enough to frost up your Y-fronts. And as we left the cottage, all noise stopped. We felt dead weird, walking the fifty yards or so to the pub. It was like at a funeral. Rows of people watching, and nobody saying a dickie-bird. It was some relief to hear the babble of voices coming from inside as Dad made with the latch to the public bar.

Everybody knows the people in North Wales are meant to be unfriendly, don't they? I mean, there's nobody in England who hasn't been told by some boring old clod that when you walk into a pub up there they all stop talking English and start talking Welsh. Well it's cobblers. They're talking Welsh all the time – it's their ruddy language. And when we walked in that pub – they all stopped. It was amazing. As Julie closed the door behind her every sound ceased. Except for the dinging of the pinball machine from the back room. It was uncanny. They all stared for what seemed like hours, never a smile. Then the babble went off again. In Welsh. All talking about us. It was horrible.

They did serve us, which was one thing – I suppose they needed the bread – and we all drank pretty fast. You do, when you're nervous. Dad looked properly sick, because this sort of thing's meant to be his job and that, and you could see him wanting to *talk* to some of them, to *explain*. Explain what, I'll leave you to imagine. Dad didn't see himself as being just like anyone else. These **Welsh gets** ought to make allowances, see – because *we* were all *right*. I told him the joke about the English bloke on holiday in North Wales, to take his mind off it. You know, the one about this geezer whose landlady tells him just to say Yakkie Dah in the local and all the Welsh'll be friendly with him. He goes in the pub every night for a week and says Yakkie Dah and nobody says a word. They just give him withering glances and go on jabbering in Welsh. He gets dead depressed.

'Are you listening, Dad? It's good this.'

He tore his eyes off the natives. You could see him itching to tell 'em he was different.

'Yes, yes, John, go on.'

'Well, on his last night he goes down the pub really fed up. Opens the door and calls out "Yakkie Dah". Nothing. Not a murmur. So he has a couple of pints and goes home. It's chucking it down, it's his last night, and he's as miserable as sin. Then just as he's turning up the lane to his digs he sees this car broke down in the road, with a bloke's legs sticking out from under. Ah well, he thinks, just one more try. Just one last attempt to be friendly. So he pokes his head under the car, in the rotten, slashing rain, and calls out: "Yakkie Dah!" And the bloke . . . and the bloke shouts back . . .'

I'd got a bit nervous by now, because I could tell lots of the locals were listening to this, although we were at a table by ourselves. I brought my voice down a notch or two. But just as I was about to give my old fellow the punchline, this grizzled old Welshman leans across. Never cracked a smile he didn't. And he said, dead loud and clear: 'Piss off, you Welsh get.'

Well of course it was terrible. I went bright red – although it *was* the punchline – and Julie looked like she'd die. Dad, though, was even worse. He gave this over-friendly, fawning smile, and joined in the laughter. Because all the Welsh were laughing, weren't they? And *he* couldn't tell they were laughing at *us*. Or wouldn't admit it. Or didn't care. It was very embarrassing. Then he said to this bloke, who'd just got a laugh at our expense. 'Can I get your table a drink? What'll you all have? I don't speak Welsh I'm afraid, I hope you speak English.' I thought Julie was going to chuck up. Anyrate we both *drank* up. And got out.

'God,' she said. 'Can't that man be a *pain* sometimes.'

The next morning, early, we got the dawn chorus. And I mean dawn. I looked at my watch, which was on the table between Julie's bed and mine, and it was just after six. The noise outside was fantastic, horrendous. Voices. Shouting, talking, catcalling. It was like twenty thousand men clocking in at a dockyard. Julie rolled over and groaned. 'Oh my God,' she said. 'They're not going to let us get away with it, are they? The swine.' I was totally dozy at that time of day. 'What?' I said. 'What you talking about? Get away with what?' She groaned again. 'Being English,' she said. 'This is for us. To ruin our holiday still more. Obviously.'

We lay there for about a quarter of an hour, listening. Only to the row, though, because it was all in Welsh, natch. Except the swearwords. They don't seem to have swearwords. They'd go jabber jabber jabber – four-letter word – gabble gabble gabble – four-letter word – jabber jabber jabber – four-letter word. Once, in a big gush of Welsh, there was a dead silence and a girl's voice said, quite plain, in her funny English: 'My old man's a *dir*ty *bugg*ah!'

By eight o'clock they'd all gone, to work, or collect the dole or whatever they do up there, but it was no good to us. We sat around the kitchen table, like wet rags, the day ruined. Dad was awful. He had a hangover you could walk a brown dog on, and he was in a dangerous mood. He even complained about the way Julie cooked breakfast – and when she suggested it might well be time he took *his* turn I thought he was going to clout her. By the time she'd mocked him for trying to suck up to the natives the night before it was clear there'd be a major row before long. I played little-boy-fourteen-year-old damn quick and suggested a ride on to Anglesey, the big island off the coast, to see the lifeboat station at Holyhead. Julie, who's no twit, said she'd go for a walk down to the lake. She's a member of a lake sailing club north of Manchester is Julie, and wanted to look at the type of boats they had here.

To be fair, it wasn't a bad day. The ships in Holyhead

29

harbour were good – I like ships – and we had a pretty good picnic with lots of meat sarnies and a couple of cans of lager each – the old fellow was being really liberated about me drinking this holiday. We met some quite friendly Welsh people, as well, which made him instantly sentimental about them again. On the drive back to the village he reckoned they weren't so bad, and one had to see their point of view, and all we had to do was get to know a few of them and we'd be accepted all right. It wasn't as if *we* were exploiting them, when all's said and done, because it wasn't *our* cottage or anything like that; we'd never dream of actually taking anything off a local: in fact we were there to spend money. Can't be bad. 'Yes, Dad,' I said meekly. 'Can't be bad at all – as long as it's your money and you spend it on me!' That night, we agreed, we'd go back to the pub. He was obviously going to go on chatting up the locals, which I didn't want to know *at all*. But I reckoned if I hung around the pinball I'd be all right. I'm pretty good at pinball, because we've got our own table at home, and Julie's not bad either. If we kept a low profile and didn't get up anyone's noses I figured we'd live.

But Julie had other plans. Say this for the Welsh, they're not slow off the mark. And as well as being racists, they're sexists too. Me and Dad were definitely treated like dirty foreigners, but in just one day Julie had got a nice little love affair sewn up. With a Welsh lad who had a dinghy. She'd been out on the lake all afternoon, slap-up lunch at the club-house, and was off to the next village to a party tonight. Little brothers *definitely* not invited. The old fellow was inclined to grumble, but he knew better than to say No. Very liberated lady, our Jules, within certain rules. And he wasn't to know she was on the Pill, was he? He didn't have a key to her bedroom bureau at home like I did. At about 7.30 this smart-looking Welsh boy arrived in a smart-looking Ford Escort, gave Dad a funny sort of leer, and Julie disappeared in a cloud of smoke. He was called Gethin, she said. Roberts, natch – they were all called Roberts. And yes, he spoke Welsh. Referred to holiday home types like us as white settlers. But for her – anything!

It was a fairly crummy night, all in all. Oh sure, I got a few games on the pinball, and a few beers, but there wasn't a lot of fun in it. They laughed at me when they won, and got all humpy when I beat them. And Welsh. Welsh Welsh Welsh, enough to drive you mad. All about me, naturally, and my Dad. They kept looking at him, and laughing, and saying 'university' and 'BMW'. Quite a number of the lads got fairly drunk, and I had to tread very careful, late on. Stopped talking altogether by about ten o'clock, for fear of getting my mouth filled if I opened it the wrong shape. Then later, when they got properly jarred, they just forgot I was there. Just swayed and jabbered, even slurring the Welsh. They seemed more interested in Dad. Much more.

He was well away. I'd heard him, a couple of times, talking about 'white settlers' and holiday homes and the economy. At first he'd only been able to get a couple of the old fogeys to listen, buying all their beer for them at that. But as the evening wore on some of the younger types had talked to him. By the time I split – about 11.20, they didn't care about closing time at all – he was surrounded. There were raised voices, and a glass got broke as people crowded round, and it looked as though Custer might be taking his last stand before long. Better off out of it, I thought. I'm only a lickle boy. Truth to tell I was staggering quite badly and I needed my bed. Fast. Something looked funny with the village as I stumbled past the BMW – the stars were on the move. I found the interior-sprung and went out like a light.

Even the dawn chorus didn't wake me next day, because I was totally spark out. When I did come round, about eight-thirty, there was an amazing row going on in the kitchen. It would have woke the dead. I lay there and listened, my head spinning, my stomach in an awful state.

It was Dad and Julie, hammer and tongs. Inevitably, she hadn't got in till three, and he'd got totally plastered and fallen over (so he said; he had a cut lip) and felt rotten. He was bawling her out for immorality, she was bawling back that he'd made us a laughing stock in the village – you know, all the usual stuff. When I crawled downstairs ten minutes later for a cup of char he was just storming out to the lav in the yard. His parting shot, over his shoulder as he left, went something like this: '. . . and I don't give tuppence for your Welsh friends. I've had them. Up to here. After last night! The veneer of civilisation, my girl, is thin – damned thin!' Then the door slammed.

Julie looked as rough as I felt. She gave me a little smile and pointed to the teapot.

'Hi, kid,' she said. 'Did you have a good—'

The door smashed open and the old fellow stood there. He was grey. He looked terrible, as if someone had banged him with a rock. He opened his mouth but he didn't seem to be able to speak. Julie stood up, looking terrified.

'Daddy,' she said.

He sat down, and gestured out the back door. I went into the lav, then stepped back smartish. They'd made a rare old mess of it, honestly. Filthy. Revolting. When I got back and told Julie, the old chap still hadn't spoken. Julie was all cut up. She seemed suddenly mad at *him*.

'That's it, you see, Daddy. This is what it *means*. This is what it *feels* like. *Now* do you understand? This is what it really *feels* like.' She stopped. Shook her head. She was almost choking. 'You and your claptrap about *caring*.' She could hardly speak. 'Your . . . your . . . claptrap.'

Father stood up like a wooden dummy. He walked over to the stairs all stiff-legged, odd. He was breathing through his nose, incredibly loudly. We heard him packing.

In a way, we didn't want to go. It felt to me too much like running out – and Julie was fraternising with the natives quite nicely, thanks very much. But one look at the old fellow's face convinced us that there was no point in arguing. In fact he looked capable of shaving her head over the Gethin thing, like girls that went with Germans during the war. We chucked our things into our bags, turned off the water and electricity, locked up the front door and went round the back to the car. Before which, actually, I popped back inside to the bedroom. It didn't take me long, what I had to do.

Round the back it was like the last act in a tragedy. Dad too grey to do anything about it, Julie giggling, out of control, nearly wetting herself. They'd let all the tyres down. And nicked the filler cap. For some reason, as he got out the foot-pump, Dad actually grinned.

'I don't think we'll bother with the police, shall we? Not a lot of point I imagine.'

I caught the mood.

'No, father,' I said solemnly. 'They'll be Welsh. The veneer of civilisation very thin, dontcher know!'

Julie was absolutely hooting with laughter now.

'That Professor Green,' she screeched. 'He's a ... he's a ... a *sociologist*! Human *behaviour*! Oh, oh, I'm going to wee myself! He's the *expert* on human relationships! Oh, oh, oh!'

Pumping up four tyres from flat cooled us down after a while, but we still kept breaking out in giggles as we set off up the narrow, dangerous road to freedom. Dad, calmer, was just glad we'd got off so lightly. They could have slashed the tyres, after all. And a filler cap's only a fiver. He did admit he didn't know what he'd said or done the night before. It could have been anything. He'd been legless.

'My God,' he said as we drove under the shadow of Snowdon. 'What a mess that place'll be in when Green goes again.'

'*If* he goes again,' said Julie. 'Serve him right anyway – ruddy white settler. Gethin said they *hate* him. *Far* worse than anyone else. He's an arrogant pig.'

I looked at Dad in the driving mirror to see what sort of mood he was in. It looked good.

'I wrote something on the bedroom wall,' I said. 'To go with Keep Wales Welsh. He'll never know it was us.'

Dad's face lost its grin, but not too much.

'What did it say?' he asked.

'Oh,' I said. 'Well. Keep Christmas White, actually. Then: Keep Newcastle Brown. Erm ... Keep Pot Black. And ... and ...'

Julie was almost bursting. So was the old fellow, although he was trying not to show it.

'And ...?' he said.

'Keep Professor Green,' I said. 'You're welcome!'

He just had time to stop in a lay-by before he became helpless. It was quite a laugh, really.

Stung

SOMEHOW OR OTHER John had got himself into a hopeless mess. After tonight's row, after Sonia had stormed out of the flat for what he hoped was positively the very last time, he decided to sort it out. He got out a two-litre bottle of their home-brewed plonk – Gibson's Genuine Gutrot it said on the label – and poured himself a half-pint glass of it. It was foul, sweetish and disgusting, tasting about as much like real wine as a mouthful of Brasso. He sat himself in front of the fire, put on a few knobs of coal to make sure it lasted for the night, and drank the glass rapidly and with determination. He was going to get his head together. He was going to put his life in order. He was going to get drunk.

After the first glass had gone down, he reached over the side of the armchair and poured himself another. The first flush of his anger had died down, and the wine – vile as it was – had made him feel a little less jumpy and ragged. He picked up the poker and carefully pushed the remains of his dinner into the hot part of the fire. It turned brown, and smoked, and slowly charred to cinders. He felt a pang of hunger in the part of his stomach not yet anaesthetised by the gutrot. He wished like hell he hadn't done it, hadn't chucked the lot on, plate and all, when Sonia had given it to him. But it served her right, it damn well served her right. Holier than thou smug bitch.

When he thought about it, most of their rows started over food. Like tonight's. She'd come in from university late – it was gone six – and immediately started moaning. What had he been doing all day? Why hadn't he gone to the department? Why couldn't he pull himself together and start work again, now, three weeks into the beginning of term? He'd told her to shut up and get him some food and she'd taken Simon into the bedroom and spent ages feeding him and changing him – which in any case is what John thought he paid the ruddy woman to do every day while she was 'looking after' the little brat.

After the baby had finally stopped screaming blue murder and gone to sleep she'd flounced into the cubbyhole they laughingly called the kitchen and started to cook. He'd switched on the portable telly and tried to watch some regional garbage programme just to get away from her nagging damn voice. But would she shut up? Would she hell. She'd got a fixation. She was absolutely obsessed. She really, genuinely, expected him to go on as if his life was still worth living, as if there was still a point in getting on with his course, working to get his degree. And when she'd gone through that, she got back on to the food. If he couldn't be bothered to work, at least he could help with the flat, the baby, the cooking. Sitting on his backside all day doing what? Too damned lazy to even have a wash. And she was doing her course, trying to catch up on a whole lost year, running a household and bringing up a baby too. And he couldn't even get a ruddy meal once in a while.

When she'd emerged from the cubbyhole at last, red in the face from heat and fury, he'd taken the plate from her, walked slowly and deliberately over to the fire, and hurled it in. Not gently, not tipped it, he'd hurled it. There'd been a terrific smash, white earthenware all over the show, and a hissing and bubbling as the mess began to burn.

John poured another big slug of the wine down his throat and stared morosely into the red heart of the fire. Sonia had said nothing. She'd just taken her meal to the table and started to eat, silently, doggedly. He'd stood by the hearth, trembling with anger, furious at her for not responding. He wanted her to scream and yell, to call him a pig and a bum and a childish, immature, selfish stoat. So he'd started in on her, in a monotonous, hurt, slightly higher-pitched than normal voice. Given her a catalogue of their woes, how it was all very well for her, how he couldn't possibly do anything creative any more, how he was trapped, hemmed in, desperate, how it was all her fault, all her fault, all her fault. She'd eaten her food, silent, then gone into the kitchen-hole and done the washing up. After that she'd come out and cleared up the bits of shattered plate and wiped off the bits of dinner that had gone over the wall. John had shut up by now, he was feeling small and stupid, sitting in his armchair. It wasn't till later that he'd managed to get the row going again, and not till much later that she'd risen to the constant baiting, started to retaliate, then to cry, then to shout at him for nagging, nagging, nagging her.

She'd shot through the door so fast in the end, and banged it so hard, that John had been caught on the hop. It wasn't for more than five minutes that he'd realised something else. She'd left Simon. She'd left him holding the baby. He could wish he'd never see her face again as much as he liked, but she'd be back. She'd left her darling baby.

For a while John had thought about going out for a drink, abandoning it. That would show the silly bitch she couldn't walk out on him like that. He'd even got his winter jacket on, because it was coming on autumn and the last few nights had been quite chilly. But he only got as far as the front door before he stopped. He hated the little pig, fair enough, but that would just be crazy. They lived in a flat that would be a death trap if a fire broke out. It was old, and crumbling, and rickety. If he left the brat and someone dropped a match somewhere, that would be that. He'd probably be done for murder.

He picked a few more knobs of coal out of the plastic bucket and arranged them where they'd burn longest with the most heat. He looked at the alarm clock, ticking noisily on the mantelpiece. She'd been gone for two hours, God only knew where. He couldn't even ring their mates to check since the telephone in the downstairs hall had been done over. He gurgled another slug into his glass and threw it down. He gave a bitter laugh, full of self-pity. What a rotten mess the whole thing was.

Thinking about the place catching fire made him smile, because it would be so easy. He looked around. The room was big, with a black-stained wooden floor scattered with little rugs. There were posters on three walls, mainly theatre posters because he was studying drama except that he'd given up out of pure apathy these days, and a large, gaudy Indian silk cover hanging from the other one. All around, on almost every flat surface, there were candles. Over in the corner, where their bed was now Simon had the other room, the candle grease – red, blue, green, you name it – was thick on the floor. Sonia was a candle fanatic. The place was an arsonist's paradise. Squalid.

It was amazing, when you thought about it, because not so long ago it had all seemed so incredibly romantic. The first night he'd ever stayed with Sonia he could hardly believe it. She'd invited him round for a meal, and they'd eaten squatting on the floor on cushions, with the light provided by a dozen candles and the music by the soft sound of a vintage Joan Armatrading LP. Put a little water with the wine! That was a laugh! They'd sat up in the gentle light, holding each other and talking, talking, talking until the early hours, drinking good cheap red out of a big bottle. Then they'd somehow made it on to the bed, and she'd somehow been naked, and so had he, and she'd taken away his virginity and they'd fallen in love. It had all been fantastic, amazing, wonderful and like nothing he'd ever even dreamed about, poor John whose Dad was in business and quite well off and fairly posh and totally, utterly, completely conventional and boring.

And Sonia was a virgin, too, and they didn't know a lot and they hadn't been madly in love for very many weeks before she was pregnant.

Damnation, thought John, half drunk now. Damnation and red hot peppers. If only I'd known then what I know now! To think I went and married her! To think we worried what our ruddy parents would think. Oh, my blistering hell.

He smiled, though, because he remembered some of the times they'd had on that big square bed. He'd been crazily in love, and Sonia was so fantastic looking. He still loved her, let's face it. Despite the rows, and the misery, and the poverty, he still loved the girl. If only it wasn't for that squalling little rat in the bedroom.

As if on cue, Simon started to whine. It wasn't loud at first, and John wasn't going to do anything about it anyway. If he wanted to squawk that was his lookout. That was up to him and his Mummy. And his Mummy wasn't home. So there. John wondered, uneasily, where the hell she was, as a matter of fact. Out getting laid? But he didn't believe it. However violently they fought, however much he managed to provoke then flatten her, she wouldn't do that. Apart from anything else she loved him. I wonder where she is in any case, though, he thought. It's getting hell's late. He hoped she wasn't round at one of their friend's house, spilling the beans about what a swine he was, painting him as black as the ace of spades. But she would be, of course, where else? It wasn't fair the way women did that. She'd be slagging him something rotten.

He listened as the crying got stronger. She'd be slagging him rotten, and it was all that little jerk's fault. If it hadn't been for him none of this would ever have happened, they'd have been in clover, they'd have been laughing. The resentment welled up in him, hot and strong. Simon

Gibson, he thought, I bloody hate you, Sonny Boy. I really bloody hate you.

Sonia had taken most of a year off from her course because of Simon, and she was trying hard to catch it up. But it was all right for her, he thought. The birth of Simon was at least something she wanted, she didn't find it screwed her up completely, not in the head. But for him, it was different. He'd lost a lot of time, the same as her, ages. But as to catching up.... It was a total, unmitigated, disaster.

The point was, John knew, that he was a very creative person. He'd thought at first he was going to be a director, but after a couple of terms he'd changed. Writing was the thing, he'd started writing plays. The more he got into it, the more he realised he was going to be famous one day. Everyone else was rubbish, the whole boiling of them. His head was bursting with ideas. He was going to be great. He would have started, as well, he would have got them down. He had, in fact; well almost. He'd almost finished his first play. And then there was Simon.

John listened to the baby screaming more uneasily. They lived in a flat, after all, and the people above and below would be wondering what the hell, no doubt of that. He made a half move out of his armchair, then flopped back again. It wasn't his problem, it just wasn't. Let the little devil wallow in it. That would show Sonia. Let the little monkey squawk. He poured himself another glass of wine and drank it carefully. It didn't taste so bad by this time, almost bearable. He giggled. He was squiffed. And there was still half the bottle to go. Apathy rules OK, he thought. Or rather, Apathy rue... That stupid bird wondered why he was apathetic. She just didn't understand what it felt like. To be a great playwright and to have it screwed up by a squalling brat. And she expected him to study! Stupid!

In the end, it was because of a play he'd seen that John

went into Simon's room. It was a play called 'Saved' – for some obscure reason – and in it a baby was stoned to death by some thugs in a park. But before the stoning, there'd been a bit in which the baby had cried, offstage, for a whole scene. And nobody had moved, nobody had lifted a finger. He remembered the play quite slowly, quite fuzzily, through his drink, and he felt rather ashamed. He was also getting worried about the neighbours, really worried. The bawling had been going on for ages.

John staggered as he turned the light on, and he staggered as he went up to the cot. Simon was lying on his back, and his face was dark from the lung power he was using to blast the cries out. He'd kicked all his covers off, and John thought for a while that he was just cold, and covered him up. But it didn't stop the squawking.

In the end he knew there was nothing else for it. He reached over the side of the cot – rather carefully, because he wasn't very steady on his feet – and picked the baby up. He felt a shiver of revulsion as its cold wet face banged against his cheek, but he forced himself to hold it, to pretend to cuddle it, leaning it over his shoulder rather like a sailor's kitbag. He jigged up and down from one foot to the other, made soothing, murmuring noises. But Simon screamed on.

John started to sing, in a soft, friendly voice. He was gritting his teeth with hatred and distaste.

'Die, you pig, you hateful
Little monster,
You hateful little tripehound,
I wish you'd ruddy die'

he sang, to the tune of Around Her Leg She Wore a Yellow Garter. But Simon didn't respond. He screamed louder if anything, and the cold tears flowed down John's face. Even his lips were cold, like two wet worms that had just crawled out of the ground. John felt something like panic start to rise.

41

'I know now,' he said. 'I ruddy know. They send 'em to prison for battering, they do, and they're crazy. I'll batter you, you snivelling little brat, I'll batter you so help me. Shut ... your ... rotten ... mouth!'

He'd yelled the last words, almost at the top of his voice. He looked at the ceiling, and panic flooded him.

'Please, Simon,' he whispered. 'Just shut your pigging gob. *Please.*'

He put the baby down and went into the kitchen cubbyhole. There was a bottle on the draining rack, with a clean teat and top in a bowl of sterilising fluid beside it. He rinsed the bottle in the fluid just to make sure, and found the powdered baby-milk in the cupboard. It was a job to read the instructions, because his eyes wouldn't focus, but he forced them to in the end because the squalling had him very frightened now. He got the bottle filled and held it under the cold tap for a while until it didn't feel too hot. Then he rushed back into the living-room, threw the last of the coal on to the fire, put the bottle down on the rug beside the wine bottle, and went to get the baby. He sat down in the chair, laid the baby across his lap, and poked the teat into his mouth.

Almost immediately, he began to suck. It was miraculous. The noise stopped as if it had been switched off. Simon's eyes rolled upwards and backwards until they looked into John's. John realised he was panting. This was awful. This was terrible. Very slowly he reached over the side of the chair until he felt his glass. He lifted it up by the rim and took a couple of big swallows. You little swine, he thought. You're ruining my life.

'Simon,' he said. 'You've scuppered me completely. You've blown it. Whatever's left between me and your Mummy is dying, kid. It's dying on its feet. You scrawny, horrible little brat you. You've scuppered me.'

Simon went on sucking. He was dressed in a white woollen smock affair, and he had long woollen socks on his feet.

His hands were bare, and he flexed his fingers all the time he drank, as if he was doing exercises.

'She's a good person, your mother,' said John. 'She's a good, nice, lovely lady. And I treat her like muck, Sonny Jim. I treat her like muck.'

Suddenly he started to cry. The tears rolled down his face but he didn't make a noise. He let out one snort but the baby stopped sucking. So he cried silentl,, rocking the child to keep it quiet, keep it drinking.

'You pig,' he said. 'You rotten little pig. You've ruined everything. What's the use of trying? What's the point of going in like Sonia does? There's nothing at the end of it any more, I'll never get a degree. I don't care, I just don't give a monkey's. There's no point.'

He sniffed, a long-drawn shuddering sniff.

'It's not just me,' he said, 'it's both of us. We're trapped. You've got us beat. We're not people any more, we're not students. I'm nineteen, Simon, nineteen miserable years old. And you've ruined everything. I couldn't care less. I just could not give a toss. About anything. At all. Any more.'

He took another gulp of drink.

'God,' he said. 'What a set-up. Crying like a baby. I'm drunk, Simon, as drunk as a lord. Oh brother! I wish I'd never seen you, kid, you'll never know how much.'

Simon had stopped sucking. His face, which had gone whiter, no longer dark from bawling, crumpled up. His knees came up to his stomach, and his hands bunched up to fists. He opened his mouth, took in a huge lungful of air, and started to scream.

This time, after about fifteen minutes, John really did get close to battering him. He tried jigging him over his back in case he had wind, he tried wrapping him in a blanket in case he was cold, he tried to *force* the teat between his gums in case it would shut him up. He kept taking large swigs of wine, and looking at the clock. It was nearly one. He was furious, consumed with anger and hate. He hated them equally, Sonia and the child. He hated them both.

Finally, defeated, he did the thing he had sworn, when Simon was born, he would never do. He put a towel on the floor, he put the baby on the towel, and he went to a drawer to get a nappy and a nappy liner.

As he fumbled, drunkenly, to unpin the dirty nappy his hatred reached its peak. He swore at Simon constantly, he called him vile, dirty, hateful things. As he unrolled the white towelling and the stench rose up from it he was almost ready to smash his fist into the tiny, blackened, face. He clenched his teeth in total revulsion as he wiped around the tiny bottom and sex organs with the soiled cloth. He wanted to be ill, he wanted not to be doing this, he wanted out. Never again, he thought, never, never again. When that bitch comes home I'm going. This is the end.

When Simon was wiped, John balled the nappy and threw it away from him. He arranged the clean nappy in a sort of triangle, doubled, as he'd seen Sonia do it, then reached for the liner and picked it up. As he did so he let out a shriek and threw it into the air. The wasp that must have been lurking in it in the drawer dropped from his finger, and crawled for the cover of the armchair bottom, too autumn-drowsy even to fly. John, enraged, forgetting Simon's half-naked, squalling body, stood and tried to stamp on it. He missed, and almost squashed the child instead. He staggered, then knelt again, furious, sucking the spot where he'd been stung. He reacted very badly to wasp stings, did John. He'd be swollen up like a football in the morning.

'You little pig,' he said. 'Now look what you've done. I've a damn good mind to ...'

He shook his head, helpless, and picked up the nappy liner from the floor. But as he was about to put it in place, he stopped, suddenly. He checked it carefully, just in case. There might be another one, a second sleepy wasp. But no.

He looked at the tiny body of his son and gave a shudder. My God, he thought, my God. If it had stung him. There. Oh, my God, how awful. With a sudden, strange, tenderness, he tucked the liner carefully into place. Then clumsily, but as best he could, he wrapped the nappy round and pinned it. The pins, as he led them carefully over his fingers, looked huge and dangerous against the soft white flesh of Simon's belly.

As if by magic, Simon stopped yelling the instant his nappy had been fixed. He lay on the towel and smiled. John, like a fool, smiled back. He picked the baby up, towel and all, and sat down in his chair. He leaned over and got his glass and took a long slow slug.

Simon opened and closed his fists. He smiled some more. He had very brown eyes. He opened his mouth and it was very wet, totally toothless, soft and gummy. He made a noise.

'Want a drink, do you?' said John. 'For God's sake finish your nosh off before you start to squall again. Here. Get your gums round that.'

As Simon sucked, he looked into John's eyes once more. John talked to him, quietly now.

'Saved your life then, Cocker, d'you know that?' he said. 'Gallantly took the blade that was meant for you. You don't know how lucky you are, kid. That wasp was almost as big as your little widdler. You'd never've played the piano again.'

He looked round the room, trying to see under the side of the chair.

'I'll get the little devil tomorrow,' he said. 'I'll hunt him down and pull his legs off one by one. Then I'll chop his head off and get it mounted and put it over your cot. As a trophy. To warn the others off!'

When his bottle was empty, Simon went to sleep. John poked at the embers of the fire with his foot and refilled his glass one-handed. As the fire crumbled, and became duller and slowly died, he watched the sleeping face. It was relaxed, at peace, the eyes twitching sometimes behind the smooth brownish lids. John tried to think, but nothing came in words. He was full of feelings, vague, weird, unknown feelings that wobbled from joyous to sad. He was studying Simon's face through a veil of tears when the door opened and Sonia walked in.

'Hi,' she said. Her voice was flat, wary. Expecting him to be fighting drunk, probably, and testing out his mood. 'What are you doing?'

'I'm crying,' said John. 'It's a free country, isn't it? I'm having a good cry with my little boy.'

There was a long pause. A piece of coal, almost ash, fell softly in the grate.

'You're drunk,' she said. She closed the door, gently, and walked slowly towards him.

'Crikey! You've changed his nappy! Look at the state of that!'

He looked. Simon was like a badly done-up parcel.

'Thanks,' said Sonia.

She leaned against the wall and looked down at him. Her face was drawn, and tired.

'Why are you crying, love?' she said. 'Are you unhappy?'

'Oh no,' said John. 'Far from it, lady.'

He looked up and gave her a crooked smile.

'I just got stung, that's all. I just got stung.'

Brutus

I'LL NEVER REALLY KNOW how it happened, to tell the truth – the killing of Brutus. Because that's what we did to him, in actual fact, although there wasn't any visible corpse for us to see and worry about; nobody stuck a knife in him, or blew his brains out. But we killed him, for sure. He never came back; no one ever saw him again in the part of town we lived in. And not surprising, neither, when you come to think about it.

The weird thing is, it all started off so simple, kind of nice. From beginning to end the business only took say three months, but in those three months my Dad had gone from being an ordinary, reasonable Joe to being a nutter almost. All over Brutus; nothing really, no one else even cared. But he got a thing about him, somehow: a fixation. Took years off his own life, I shouldn't wonder. The hatred in him was awful, it kind of ate into him. He used to shake.

Which is sad, I can tell you, because my Dad's a placid sort of bloke a lot of the time. I mean he's dead strict, and he used to thump the old lady sometimes when I was younger, when he'd been on the blind. It didn't do to cross him, neither, when he had a certain look in his eye. But generally he was pretty easy-going. Never had no enemies at work or round about. Everyone liked him and he got on with everyone. He didn't even have a thing about blacks and Pakis like some folk do, and when the Sylvesters moved in to the end terrace he didn't bat an eyelid. He even laughed

47

at some folk who started muttering about it bringing the house prices down and all that. 'Silly sods,' he'd say. 'Anyone who could bring the prices down in this dump any lower would have to be from outer Space.'

Truth to tell, it is a bit of a dump where we live. It's right on the edge of the town – which isn't a very posh one anyway – and behind it are the Yorkshire moors, running straight over the top into Yorkshire itself, where all the queer folk live. But it's not an estate, see, and that's what makes it special. Not crummy 'thirties houses, or modern egg-box things. It's an old village, with its own name, and its own pubs and lots of the old devils still tottering around that've lived here for a hundred and ninety years. The accent they use is amazing: so thick you could cut it with a knife. It is part of the town, like, but it's not surrounded, on account of the moors, and it's a pretty quiet, friendly little place. It's called Mooredge.

I'm not making a lot of sense here, I reckon, saying it's a bit of a dump then cracking it up to be summat special. But it's both. All the houses are old, thick stone walls and sagging roofs with stone slates that weigh a ton each, and it's scruffy. But folk care. Everyone knows everyone else and everyone keeps up his patch of garden if he fancies and doesn't if he can't be bothered, and it's dead nice. And quiet.

For most folk, when the Sylvesters moved in, the quiet was the main worry, like. I mean some of them, especially the older ones who'd not seen a lot, didn't like the idea of any blacks coming there anyway, as if they actually were from outer Space, or summat. But most folk up our way are pretty used to seeing them around, and didn't bother all that much. Didn't expect to get murdered, if you know what I mean. But there was a lot of fear about the noise. They were West Indians, the Sylvesters, and they spoke like it. Their accent was even funnier than the Mooredge one. And people thought they might be playing this Reggie (as they called it) all hours of the night. And lifting all the old oil drums off the edge of the moors, like, and turning themselves into a steel band. Crazy.

As it turned out, for such a big family, they were very quiet. I'm still not sure exactly how many there are of them, because there was a divorce or something in the question, and the number of kids tended to go up and down a little, depending on who had who at the weekends, and such. But there was at least six – Mum and Dad and four kids, ranging from about eight years old to getting on for twenty. I'm nearly sixteen myself, and there weren't none of 'em exactly around my age. Not that I'd have palled up with 'em anyway I reckon. I've got plenty of mates already, see, and I'm kept pretty tied up what with the Air Training Corps and such.

So that was that. For the first couple of weeks they were there, no problems. Sometimes there'd be six or so of 'em, sometimes eight or ten. Always a couple of battered old cars outside, because one of the sons was a mad mechanic, but they never said boo to a goose. Even the crusty old devils who even hated Yorkshire folk – we were just in Lancashire, see, and it was a matter of life and death to some of 'em – got used to them, and could be caught-out smiling back when one of these big ebonies flashed all their ivories in a grin. They were all in work, those of them old enough, so no one could accuse them of being a burden on the State or whatever the phrase is, they didn't kill goats in the front garden and drink their blood, they kept the windows shut and switched off the telly at close-down just like everyone else, they were clean, neat and normal. Even anyone who'd wanted to hate them – and there must have been those, I guess, it's a free country – would have been hard put to find a peg to hang it on. All in all, on the good neighbour stakes, they had it made.

Until, that is, Brutus appeared on the scene.

I can't remember for sure just how long it was after

they'd moved in that he appeared, but I think it was under a month. And all the good work they'd done in that month — the mechanic boy had properly got on Dad's right side by putting something right under the bonnet of our old jalopy, for instance — it all went out the window. For my father, it happened literally overnight.

The trouble was, see, Dad works nights. He's down at one of the big textile mills in town, and I'm not sure what he does, but he's in charge of quite a few men I think. He works long hours for not a lot of money — textiles is a raving disaster area these days as you probably know — and he's worked nights for donkeys years. They have to work twenty-four hours a day just to keep the mill above water. So when this dirty big dog turned up on the scene during one of the Sylvesters' family reshuffles one weekend, it had an effect on him that was amazing.

What is it about West Indians? Is it true they're noisier than other folk? Are they all deaf or what? Is it that it's noisy in the jungle where they live up trees — as some people say — so don't mind a row? No, I'm beginning to sound like me Dad got to sound now. But honest to God, Brutus even got on my nerves after a while, and I sleep like a log.

Problem was, they just didn't seem to have noticed what a quiet place Mooredge is. I mean, plenty of folk have got dogs, and that, but apart from the odd flurry, usually in the afternoon, you almost never hear 'em. They're not a nuisance, not let to bark and yowl all the hours God sent. Nobody's ever said to anybody 'Keep your ruddy dog quiet', but folk seem to know. It's unheard of to leave one out at night, in the yard, say, just barking. It's just not on. Apart from anything else, there's sheep all over the moors at back of the village, and if a farmer catches a dog worrying, it's out with a shotgun and blam! All legal and above board. Not that Brutus ever bothered with sheep, even the times when he was let to roam. Preferred to stay in the

50

comfort of his own patch of garden. And drive my old man nuts.

The first time it happened we didn't even know it was their dog, of course. It was just that from about eight o'clock in the morning this great booming bark started up. I was downstairs getting my breakfast before I went to school, and me Dad had been in his kip for about an hour. Mum damn nearly dropped her cup of tea down her pinny.

'Ee 'eck,' she said. 'That were on like that till gone twelve o'clock last night. If it wakes your Dad there'll be ructions.'

No 'if' about it. Ten minutes later he was braying on the bedroom floor with his boot heel till we thought he'd have the plaster down.

'Molly!' he shouted. 'Go and see what that ruddy row is. Take a ruddy wallbrick and smash its ruddy skull in. If *I* catch it I will!'

We looked at each other, across the kitchen table.

'Ee, Trev,' she said. 'Will you be a good lad and go and 'ave a look for us? He'll kill me else.'

Judging by the tone of me Dad's voice I reckon she had a point. I got on me jacket and pludged out. It was a lovely morning, with a good warm breeze blowing down off the moors. But that dog! It didn't take me long to see where the noise was coming from.

He was standing in the front garden of the Sylvesters and he was a right big creature. I don't know what sort you'd've called him – it looked like a bit of several. He was as big as an alsatian though, with this dirty big mouth. He was opening it good and wide, and his whole body gave a spasm every time he let one go. They were real deep, and you could hear them echoing round the moors. If anyone was going to batter this one's skull in, it wasn't going to be me, no danger. He was a monster.

I stood there like a fool for a couple of minutes wondering what to do. I wandered up to the gate, casual-like, as if I

51

was just strolling and wanted to see the pretty doggie. As I got closer the barks came thicker and faster. The effort he put into it, you'd have thought he could have knocked you over just with the noise and force of his breath. It was daft. To make him slow down I had to go away, and to make him stop altogether I was going to have to do something else again. But what? No way was I walking past him to bray on the front door; no way! He was tied to a bush right enough, on a piece of grey, weak-looking clothes-line stuff. But one, I didn't know how long it was, and two, it looked about strong enough to hold a kitten. A *weak* kitten.

Inspiration comes to him that waits, and it wasn't long before Albert Einstein (me) nipped round the back. And that was the time for a real surprise. Because bray as I might, I got no reply. Just a sort of mad explosion of monster barks from the front garden. They'd gone out. And as they were *all* gone, Mum and youngest kids included, it had to be for the day. One of the old bangers was missing sure enough. They'd gone on a trip – and bang had gone me Dad's beauty sleep!

That night, when me Dad had gone off to work, looking like Death and twice as unfriendly, it fell on me to be the bearer of the glad tidings to the Sylvester family. I still don't know to this day why he couldn't've done his own dirty work, because his reasons sounded more like excuses to me. In fact it was Mum he told to go and see 'em, but that would've been a complete hoot. My Mum's about the meekest person I've ever met in me life – something to do with living with me Dad for twenty years I expect – and the idea of her complaining is just too ridiculous. She'd've had a heart-attack straight off.

'But Ted,' she said, going all pale-like. 'Why don't *you* tell them, dear? It would sound much better coming from you, surely?'

'I can't tell 'em, Molly, how can I? I'd lose me rag, that's all, and I'd boot that big black so-and-so from here to

52

breakfast. By, I'd like to get me hands round his throat, the noisy get.'

Crikey, I thought. Didn't take old man Sylvester long to turn into a *black* so-and-so! Good job the dog's pale brown!

'But Ted, are you . . . I mean . . . Oh. Heck.'

Ah well, I thought, here we go.

'I'll go, Dad,' I said. 'If you're too scared to do your own dir—' Something about the way his eyes went stopped me. Whoops! You don't talk to my Dad like that when he's had no kip. 'Hey, only joking, our Dad,' I said hurriedly. 'You're dead right – no point in starting a row.'

He growled.

'Don't know about a row,' he said. 'But you just tell that monkey that if it happens again there'll be trouble. Big trouble.'

As you can imagine, I felt a bit weak at the knees going in. There was no sign of the dog, so I used the front door, expecting I don't know what to happen. The lady came, the Mum, and gave me a right friendly smile, all teeth and eye-whites. And ten seconds later I was sitting at the table with half the family and a big mug of tea in me mitt. It was ridiculous. You can't have a row when they treat you like that. I even stroked the ruddy dog!

But when it came to it I gritted my teeth and spat it out. How me Dad was a night worker, and how it was such a quiet place with the moors and that, and how he'd only got about an hour last night. They took it very nice, and I got so confident after a while that I cracked up about what an ogre he was, and how frightened me Mum was of him. I went a teeny bit over the top, I guess. Almost brought tears to me eyes. I half expected a round of applause when I'd finished. But they all sat there nodding, very serious. And apologised. And said it wouldn't happen again.

'Oh,' I said, half stunned I suppose. 'Oh. Oh, well . . . Thanks!' And two minutes later I was back at home. Feeling a right fool.

The problem was, it didn't happen. Oh it was fine for a few days. That whole week in fact. He barked some in the evenings, but nobody seemed to mind about that, least of all me Dad, who was at work, but the mornings were fine. Then, after about ten days, he set up his row, about quarter to eight. After five minutes the old man was braying on the floor with his boot, after ten he was downstairs terrorising the old Mum to go out and slaughter the dog, or the family, or both, with her bare hands, and in the silence after his shouting spree I noticed through Mum's tears that Brutus had stopped. The father went upstairs again, and he must've gone to sleep that time, because he looked all right later. But three days later it happened again, just for five minutes this time, then a few days after that yet again. And inevitably, me Dad got to the stage that because he knew it *might* happen, he lay awake expecting it. He wasn't kidding, either, you could see he wasn't sleeping right. It was crazy, stupid. It was getting to be a proper worry.

I did go back again, to the Sylvesters' – I had to, I didn't get a choice. In fact I went back three times. Every time they were as nice as pie, and I began to suss things out a little. At first they said it was an accident, then they said well of course the dog had to be let out for a morning pee and they couldn't always stop it giving a bark or two, then they started to get a shade ratty themselves. What it was in actual fact, I think, was that Mrs Sylvester was just a natural scatterbrain. I've got an auntie like it, Aunt Maud. She's nice, and easy-going, and she just takes life as it comes. Her house is a tip, she doesn't give a damn, and if she says she'll see you on Tuesday week she turns up on Wednesday fortnight. This Mrs Sylvester lady – nice, friendly, a good laugh obviously – just didn't always remember. Coming from somewhere where maybe all the dogs barked all the time, she probably didn't even notice. She probably just thought me Dad was a moaning twit who ought to stuff cotton wool in his ear'oles. But in spite of it she tried, she truly tried. But sometimes she forgot.

I tried to explain this to me Dad but it was a waste of time. He wasn't interested in their side any more. He was building up a sort of head of steam of hatred that got quite frightening, and he'd begun to brood as well. He used to mutter on about ways of getting rid of the dog, of killing it. And he was serious, I swear. He actually got a book out of the library called Malay Charms and Poisons, and started asking blokes in the pub if paraquat tasted of anything and if you could get cyanide in tablets to hide in chunks of meat – like a Bob Martins only different! If it hadn't been so worrying it could have been dead funny. But he meant it, the poor old get. I felt right sorry for him.

And the race thing, too. He got this fixation about the Sylvesters being black. It was all because they were black that this had happened. It was like a sick joke. He reckoned to me one day that they wouldn't miss the dog because they'd probably only bought it for meat and then found they couldn't eat it in this country. He seemed to mean it; it was pathetic. I mean, apart from anything else the Sylvesters loved the dog, they were wild about it, especially the kids. He began to hate the other neighbours, as well, because they didn't care. The dog didn't worry them, working days, and anyway, most folk had proper taken to the family.

Then one morning, about eight o'clock, there was this terrible scene. Mrs Sylvester had forgot about me Dad again – although it was the first time for at least a week – and Brutus had started off barking. Mum and me froze at the kitchen table expecting the boot-heel job, when all of a sudden me Dad appears in his shirt-tails and trousers – back-to-front. He was black in the face with rage, had no shoes on, his hands holding his crazy breeks up and sort of groaning with anger. He gave us a wild look then shot out of the front door. I shot after him to try and stop him, but it was no good at all. Mrs Sylvester must have seen him slamming through their front gate – he didn't mind about the dog because it had turned out it was a right soft creature – and she opened the front door with a kind of scared smile. She called out, 'Brutus. You come in here, you wicked dog,' when the father let fly. It was terrible, honest. He insulted her up hill and down dale, called her a fat black bitch, all sorts. I just stood there, by the gate, red as a beet, trying not to hear it. I was shamed, I don't mind admitting it. Proper shamed. It's a pity none of the big sons were in, or the old feller, so's they could have knocked him over. He surely had it coming to him, no danger. He ended up telling her if it happened again he'd be taking the law into his own hands with a vengeance. Then he came home. He was grey. He looked totally knackered. He went upstairs without a word. A while later I went down to see Mrs Sylvester and apologise. She was pretty upset but she give me a cup of char just the same. A right nice lady, in any language.

Nothing happened, which was the weirdest. She must either of not told her old feller about me Dad, or told him it wasn't so bad, or summat. There was no braying on the door, no punch-up, no row. You'd've thought me Dad would've been relieved, would've thanked his lucky stars to get off so light, but he just got worse. And about a week later, he sprung his plan to me. To get rid of Brutus.

I still feel so bad about it, I'd rather not tell. Perhaps I should've been stronger, tried harder to persuade him out of it, I don't know. I did try to pretend I thought he was joking at first, I even dared a laugh at him. But it was no good. He had a strange look to him, he was sort of half-mad. Just on this point, mark you, nothing else. But there couldn't be any argument when it came down to it. He had this plan and he needed me to help him. I'm his son, so that's that. You can't let your own father down, can you? Even if he's up the creek.

It was a simple plan, and as easy as pie to do. We waited

till one afternoon when Mrs Sylvester and the kids had gone to town shopping, then me Dad got the old jalopy up one of the moor tracks a couple of hundred yards off the edge of the village. I had a jolly good look around our street to make sure none of the neighbours were about, or looking out of their windows, then popped into the Sylvesters' garden and broke the old clothes-line round Brutus's neck. Then I went out again, got down behind a garage out of eyesight of the neighbours, and waited till the daft dog came snuffling out the front gate into the road. Then, see, if anyone told Mrs S I'd been in the garden I could say I'd gone to knock on the door, have a cup of char or summat, and there'd been no one in. Brutus had been there, right as ninepence, hitched up to his bush.

I suppose it was four or five minutes before he came out, no more. He looked up and down, deciding which way to wander, and I gave him a dead soft call. Up went his ears, then his head, and ten seconds later we were romping up the lane together. Two hundred yards, grab his collar, open goes the back door of the car, and in goes Brutus. He must have thought it was treats time, a ride in a car and all. I gave him some boiled sweets to make up for what we were going to do to him.

On the way I will say for myself that I tried to persuade me Dad again. I told him we had no right, I told him it was stealing, I told him it would break the kiddies' hearts. He just sat behind the wheel and drove, his face as hard as rock. 'Hurt the kiddies, my foot,' he muttered. 'Little they'll care, you'll see. You're getting dead soft, our Trevor.' He changed down a gear as we got to a steep part of the road, on the way up towards the M62. 'Anyway,' he said. 'We're being kind to him this way. We're not going to kill him or nowt like that. It's an act of mercy, the way those so-and-sos look after him. They're not fit to keep cockroaches, never mind a dog.'

'Kind!' I half whistled. Phew!

'Yeah,' he said, grinding his voice out between his teeth. He was proper mad at me, near the point where he'd start thumping. 'They don't give a bugger for it, it stands to reason. Out all hours of the day and night, rain, shine or snow. They probably don't even feed it right. They don't deserve to keep it. It's a fact. They don't know how to treat a dog. Terrible.'

I bit my lip to keep my mouth shut. If he could *hear* himself! *They* didn't know how to treat a dog! And him just driving off to. . . I bit my lip and made myself watch the scenery.

It's fantastic it is, the scenery up on the high moors. But the trouble is, it's fantastically lonely. I didn't know how far we were going to go, but already it was lonely. That poor ruddy dog. But when we actually turned on to the M62 and headed for Leeds, an even worse thought hit me.

'Not on the motorway, Dad!' I said. 'Not with all this traffic! Come on, Dad, be fair! Not on the motorway!'

I guessed from the way he denied it so strong that that's what had been in his mind. The M62 is one of the busiest motorways you've ever seen, it's amazing. All the trucks in the world seem to be on it, all the traffic between Lancashire and Yorkshire and Leeds and Hull and Liverpool. If he dropped Brutus there he'd have no chance, no chance at all. He'd be dead in a second, crushed, mangled, minced. There'd be blood and fur for miles around. And people do it, I know that. People drop their unwanted dogs on motorways, then chug off home and have a drink. It's true. It's bloody true.

'Can't do it on the motorway anyway,' he said angrily. 'Some interfering pig'd get our number. It's just the distance, that's all. I don't know how good their sense of direction is, damned if I do.'

I almost had to laugh. You'd've thought the ruddy dog was superhuman. We'd come near twelve miles already. But we'd come off the motorway on to the bleakest part of the moors about thirty miles before me father was satisfied. He pulled her up and we sat there with the window open. The wind was fresh and lovely, and it was eerie and quiet. Hardly a bird singing. Brutus, the noisy Brutus, was asleep on the back seat. And all around us, some quite close, some nibbling away up the sides of the moors, were sheep. That a starving dog would start to chase. That a farmer with a gun owned. A farmer with a gun.

'Don't do it, Dad,' I said, sudden-like. 'Please. Don't do it.'

His face went set. He gave me a glare. In ten seconds flat he'd opened the door, bundled the dog out, and started her up. The collar, which I'd taken off earlier, he chucked out after. He shot off like a rocket, bouncing and bucketing over this stony track back to the main road. I had a look round after a half a mile, I couldn't stop myself. Brutus was about a hundred yards behind, standing still, panting fit to bust. He looked puzzled, although that's daft I guess. He'd run himself out.

You bastard, I thought, about me Dad. You rotten bastard. I didn't feel sorry for him any more. I loathed him. And I didn't feel too great about myself. But what could I do?

If they ever suspected it was us that had got rid of Brutus, the Sylvesters never mentioned it. And they never got another dog, neither, which at least would've been poetic justice. Come to that, it would've been funny enough if me Dad had suddenly been put on days. But he stayed on nights, and started to sleep proper again, and became a normal, reasonable Joe just like before. Which just goes to show.

But I never got a cup of char with Mrs Sylvester again, that's for sure. A pity, that, a proper pity. A rotten, stinking shame.

At the Sign of the Sack of Spuds

PETER MCTAGGART, at eighteen years old and a third-generation Irish immigrant, took himself, his country, and his education very seriously. He'd chosen the university he went to for one thing and one thing only – its reputation as the best place in England to learn Irish. Because despite the warnings he'd had from his Uncle Des, who had a little of the Gaelic left himself and swore it was a divvil of a language to get the hang of, especially when it came to putting it down on paper, he was determined to do just that. What the hell use he thought it was going to do him back home in Hull, nobody had the faintest idea. But he was taking a couple of other subjects as well, so it didn't matter much.

What did shake him, though, because he took it all so seriously, was the advice his professor gave him after the third or fourth session. They'd been working on basic pronunciation, which involved a queer process. The professor would make the sounds that had to be made – and very strange they sounded, to Peter's native English ears – and while he was doing it, he'd spray an aerosol of charcoal down his throat. Then Peter had to get his head up close, and stare into the professor's mouth, and see exactly where the pink bits were, and exactly where the black. That way he could work out which parts the tongue had touched, how close the professor's mouth had closed to make a sound, and so on. When *he* tried to reproduce the sound he had to memorise the movement inside his mouth, and after a couple of goes *he'd* get the charcoal treatment so that his gob could be examined to see where he'd gone wrong. They used mirrors, as well, and all in all if anyone had blundered into the room they'd probably both have been arrested.

After about an hour, when they were drinking a cup of coffee to get the charcoal out of their tubes (the Prof was a pretty basic sort of fellow, and actually spat into his waste-bin) he leaned across and said to Peter: 'You know, McTaggart, there's a pub you ought to drink in. Do you the world of good. Do you drink at all?'

Peter blushed, because it seemed so strange.

'I . . . Well, not a lot,' he said. 'I've never bothered much.'

'Ah,' said the Prof. 'Pity that. I can't take you myself because I'm an alcoholic. Can't go near a pub in case I break out. Pity.'

Peter's face was like fire. Crikey, he thought, a couple of months ago I was at school. Now here I am sitting in a university with a raving nutter who gobs in the wastebasket and tells me his innermost secrets. He tried to imagine talking to a schoolteacher like that. But he couldn't.

The professor let out a laugh.

'I'd better explain,' he said. 'I'm not trying to put you on the Primrose Path to ruin that I tripped down so lightly, many years ago. There's actually a good reason to go to this pub. You see . . .' He stopped and smiled. 'No, I won't tell you. If you take a drink, try it. It's only just off the campus. One of the few places the authorities didn't knock down when they started to expand this fun palace. The locals got up a petition.' He gestured vaguely out of the window at the jungle of concrete monstrosities. 'All that lot,' he said. 'That modern *architecture*. It's only been here since the early seventies. Six thousand students to eighteen thousand, in ten years, this place has gone. The locals call it Butlins – you try, next time you're on a bus. Ask for Butlins. In 1972

61

that lot was still houses, hundreds of reasonable brick terraced houses. It was the Irish quarter.'

On the quiet, Peter thought he was nuts, or had been secretly hitting the bottle again. But that evening, with nothing better to do than go back to the lonely student village, he went to the pub. It was an odd place, a brick Victorian building with a painted front and bare, ragged bricks at the back and sides where everything else had been pulled down. It was like an island of real building in a sea of deadly concrete. Although he wasn't a big pub man, it made him feel good to look at. It was called the Ducie.

It was early when he went in, about quarter past six, and there didn't appear to be any customers. There was a little lobby affair leading to the bar, a door off to the left, another door on the right, and one farther inside marked 'Private – Beware of the Dog' which he later learned was to deter burglars, because there wasn't a dog after all. Behind the bar, reading the evening paper on a high stool, was a friendly looking small woman, with black curly hair. She put her paper down as he approached and gave him a smile.

'Hello, love,' she said. 'What're you havin'?' She was as Irish as it was possible to be.

He was far too shy to try and get up a conversation, so he just ordered a half of mild and hung about. There was an electric fan heater behind the bar, but it was cold enough in front of it. When the landlady had taken his money she gave another smile and said: 'Get over there in the little room, why don't you? It's the only one where I've got the fire lit, till Eamon comes back with a bag of that coal from the shop. We've had no delivery. There's a couple of the working lads in there, but you won't mind them.'

She indicated one of the doors and Peter headed for it. Inside it was tiny, much too small for the dartboard it had in to be of much use. There was a coal fire half up the chimney, and two enormous men were huddled over it, smoking cigarettes. They had on donkey jackets and torn trousers that were covered in mud. Their boots were practically invisible, they were so thick in it. As he perched down on a wooden bench, behind a round table with cast-iron legs, one of the men nodded a massive, beefy head, and told Peter: 'Evening. A raw night.' Peter blushed, and nodded. The two men looked into the flames, silent. Until after a few minutes, in which his own nervous breathing was the only sound Peter was conscious of, they started to talk quietly to each other. It dawned on him very slowly that they were talking Irish.

Over the next few weeks Peter went to the pub every evening he got the chance – which was almost every evening – and a lot of lunchtimes, late or early. A fair number of students from the English department, where he was doing a subsidiary, were regulars, and he palled up with some of them. He was very soon on nodding terms with Kathleen, the landlady, and Eamon, her husband, and before much longer on chatting terms. She treated some of the students like real friends – sons almost – and provided hot evening meals at the bar for those who lived alone in grotty flats and hadn't managed to get hitched up with girls old-fashioned enough to do all their cooking and dirty work as well as sleeping with them. He graduated from halves of mild to pints of bitter in double-quick time, and had a couple of very heavy sessions indeed when Eamon – who hated closing time – kept them on afterwards and opened a bottle of poteen, the raw, illegally distilled spirit he got in lemonade bottles 'from a man over in Mayo'.

Unlike most of the students, though, Peter never lost his seriousness – over his subject, his aims in life, anything. He took Irish so seriously that he never actually admitted to anyone for a long time that he was taking it, for fear of being laughed at. He listened to the handful of working men – most of them labouring on the new motorway – who sat and chatted in Gaelic, and he let on to Kathleen once that although his family had lived in Hull for years and he spoke

63

with a Hull accent, he felt as Irish as she was and intended always to stay so. Kathleen, who'd come over from Kerry just after the war, when Eamon, the drunken bletherer, had thought to make his fortune in scrap, agreed that it was the only thing to do. She still had most of her brothers and sisters over there – and so did Eamon – and they still went on a visit at least every year.

'England's all right, mind,' she said. 'But it's not the old country and it never will be, if you know what I mean.'

As well as listening to Irish more times than he'd have believed possible in the centre of Northern England, Peter also, in the Ducie, had to listen to Irish jokes. His reaction was always one of annoyance, and disgust that anyone should be so racist. Of course the Irish weren't stupid, they were exactly the same as anyone else. But when he tried to complain to his friends, or have a serious argument about it, they just laughed and called him a prig. (And worse, of course, when the respectable old lady regulars weren't in earshot.) The craziest thing of all, which he could never come to terms with, was that Kathleen was the main culprit. She loved Irish jokes, the dafter the better, and when she told them all the one about the Irish sending a rocket to the sun – instead of just the moon – to beat the Russians and Yanks, but waiting till dark so that it didn't melt, she almost laughed herself into a fit. One day Alan, one of the English department students, offered what he called complete proof. He wrote on one side of a piece of cardboard: 'How to keep an Irishman amused for hours. PTO.' And on the other side he wrote the same thing. Then he gave it to Kathleen.

There were about seven of them in the snug, including Peter, and they watched fascinated. Kathleen took the card, read the words, turned it over, read the words, turned it over, read the words, turned it over, read the words, turned it over ... Then she looked at Alan with sparkling eyes, handed it back, and told him: 'Ach, Alan! You'll have

me at this all the afternoon!' And burst into *peals* of
delighted laughter. Peter didn't know whether to smile or
get depressed. He was only glad he'd never told his friends
just how he felt about being Irish – or indeed, that in the
language he was so shiftily learning McTaggart meant 'Son
of the priest'. They'd have torn him to pieces with their
humour.

Finally, when he'd known Kathleen for a good long time,
he confessed that he was studying Irish, and why. Far from
mocking, as he'd half expected, she was quite chuffed. She
chatted on for a good while about her girlhood, and how the
language was dying out in the part she'd lived in, although
it was on the edge of the gaeltacht, and tried the few phrases
– mostly to do with drink – that she heard from the motorway labourers now and again. After they'd been talking for
more than half an hour, she sat bolt upright, snapped her
fingers, and looked at him wide-eyed.

'Mrs O'Rourke!' she said.

Peter waited politely. No point in rushing Kathleen.

'Now where are you living now, Peter love?' she said at
last. 'In some nasty dirty little hole it'll be I suppose. Or
that student village, so dear it's shameful and such horrible
food I wouldn't give to a pig or Eamon! You'll want to go to
Mrs O'Rourke! You'd bring a bit of class to the place,
though you needn't say I said it!'

'Sorry,' said Peter. 'Who's Mrs O'Rourke?'

'Oh, you'll not know the old trout. She's a widow woman
who drinks in the Carrion Crow. But Peter! God bless you,
she lets out rooms!'

He still looked puzzled. Eamon, who'd been half dozing
by the fire, spoke without lifting his head or opening his
eyes.

'She'll spit it out in a minute or two, Peter,' he said. 'If
you're in no hurry, like. The fact of the matter is, Mrs
O'Rourke runs a Gaelic house. The whole boiling speaks it,
it's like a bloody madhouse, so it is.'

'That's right, love,' said Kathleen placidly. 'And all her lodgers, also. She likes to feel at home in the midst of all. Now all these working lads you see in here, the motorway men, the half of them is staying with Mrs O'Rourke. Will I have a little word with her for you, like?'

When Peter told his professor he was moving into a Gaelic house he laughed.

'That'll be old Mother O'Rourke,' he said. 'It's taken you long enough to find out, McTaggart. But I see you've grown a beer belly, that's one thing. You need to be in training.'

Peter's eyes were round with indignation. The professor laughed out loud.

'Think I should have told you myself, do you, Sunshine?' he said. 'Well I shouldn't. You like to booze now, do you? Eamon and Kathleen given you the taste? Mother O'Rourke's, young feller, will make your eyes stick out like chapel hat-pegs. Do you like murphies?'

No reply. The professor rolled his eyes.

'Oh my God,' he said. 'Just how well brought up can you be! Spuds, lad. Praties. Tatties. Know what they are? Potatoes. Do you like them?'

'Of course I like them,' replied Peter coldly. 'In moderation. I mean, I don't eat more than anyone else. They're just a ... Well, they're potatoes. They're all right.'

'Have you ever heard of the bogs?' the Prof went on. 'The bog Irish? The far West?' He sighed. 'Look, McTaggart,' he said. 'I know you've got this thing about the Irish, about being Irish, this romantic thing, but—'

'Oh, look here,' Peter began. He was red to the roots of his hair. The professor raised his hand, then dropped it.

'All right, sorry,' he said. 'I was Irish once, remember that. But these motorway rednecks, these navvies, these wandering labourers. They're a special breed, McTaggart. Just because they speak the language doesn't make them

66

any *more* Irish. You wouldn't go to a dosshouse full of *Scottish* roadmen, would you? They're a different breed.'

Peter summoned up all the dignity he had in him.

'For a teacher of Celtic languages, you seem to be remarkably intolerant of the Celtic races,' he said. It sounded priggish even to him. Dreadful.

The professor looked at him, almost sadly.

'I'm not trying to be funny, or even to warn you off,' he said. 'You have a natural aptitude for this language, and being among native speakers will be extremely valuable for you. There are other ways of doing it, but there's nothing wrong with this way. As *long* as you go in with your eyes open. I'll just say this: old Mother O'Rourke's dosshouse is known to some as The Sign of the Sack of Spuds. Try not to get hurt.'

He stood up. Peter did too. The class was over. He was completely confused.

The professor opened the door.

'Cheer up, McTaggart,' he said, smiling. 'Just keep an open mind, that's all. And if you get into trouble, for God's sake come and tell me. Or Kathleen, if you prefer. But don't hesitate to tell someone. Good luck.'

Crikey, thought Peter miserably, as he walked down the superheated concrete passageway. What the heck have I let myself in for?

Strangely enough, after her first enthusiasm, Kathleen had cooled on the idea of Mrs O'Rourke's as well. But her back-pedalling was a red rag to a bull, especially as she was even more evasive than the Prof had been when Peter tried to press for reasons. He pestered and badgered her until she finally did speak to Mrs O'Rourke, then he went around and gave her a month's rent in advance the same afternoon – in cash. The deal was well and truly clinched. And Kathleen, when he told her, just shrugged and told him: 'Ah well, you'll do all right I suppose. You're one of the lads and have had a drink often enough with the most of them.'

Peter didn't have a lot of gear to move, more or less a bag of clothes, a box of books and his record player. Alan dropped him off in his car, and he rang the bell. After a while he banged on the door with his fist, remembering from his last visit that the bell didn't work. As Alan's old banger disappeared down the dirty street of smoke-blackened red-brick Victorian houses, he felt a twinge of something like panic. The car was hardly up to date, but at least it was twentieth century. The road itself had an air of ancient decay, with smashed street-lamps, blowing garbage, and a few black kids playing hop-scotch on the corner. Mrs O'Rourke, the forbidding widow-woman, was hardly reassuring. She opened the door, gestured him in without a word, and stood aside while he humped the record-player over the threshold. It was dark in there, and there were several large sacks in the passage that he hadn't noticed when he'd fisted her his advance rent on the door-step two days before. She had not, then, invited him to enter.

'Mind the praties,' she said. 'And that music box you've got there. No playing of it till all hours now. We've respect-able working men in this house, my lad, and they've to get their sleep. The man comes to fetch them off to their work at six a.m. in the morning. Top of the stairs and turn right's where you're staying. Himself is not at home now so shift your gear in. The dinner's at seven thirty sharp, and if you're not there at all you misses it.'

It had not occurred to Peter that he was sharing, but that's who 'Himself' turned out to be – a room-mate. The room itself was small, and not clean, with a worn carpet and two tiny beds. There was a fire grate with cold ashes in it – so that was how they got their heat. There was a bucket of coal and a pile of torn paper and some broken furniture for kindling. The room smelled pretty bad to him. Of socks, and damp, dirty clothes. He crammed most of his gear under the bed, amid the piles of fluff. There didn't seem to be anywhere else. He felt a desperate urge to run round to Kathleen already. God Almighty. What *had* he let himself in for?

Seven thirty for the evening meal was a carefully-chosen time. It just gave the other lodgers time for a few pints of Guinness after the vans had brought them back from the motorway or wherever, and after they'd got the food down – a process that took much less than twenty minutes – they could be back in the pub with a clear two and a half hours drinking time, even if the landlord was strict about the law. There were seven other men in the house, plus Mrs O'Rourke and her son, an ill-looking boy of about fourteen. Peter couldn't imagine where they all fitted in, because apart from anything else they were enormous. Huge country men, who wore bulky clothes – ragged sweaters with leather belts round the outside, filthy trousers and mud-caked boots of leather or rubber. He recognised three of them from the Ducie, and they nodded shyly. Everyone got tongue-tied, especially when he told them – in Irish – that he spoke a little of the language – the Kerry branch, which was theirs – and wanted them not to speak to him in English at all. In the event, what with the shyness and the speed at which they got the food disposed of, hardly twenty words were spoken.

The meal, to Peter's educated palate, was unbearable. There was indeed meat – it looked like some sort of steak – but it had been boiled. There was no salt on the table, and none had gone into the water either – it was like wet cardboard. There was a spoonful of limp cabbage, boiled to a pulp, and a mountain of potatoes. They too were boiled, they too were unsalted. The quantities were enormous, and by the time the men had finished, Peter had hardly made a dent in his. He looked helplessly at Mrs O'Rourke, but her glance back was stony. He claimed not to be hungry, and the plate was snatched away in a furious flurry. There was no pudding, no afters of any sort. As their plates were

69

mopped clean with their bread, the men stood up, still chewing, mumbled something to the hostess, and left. It was as bad as that. Peter stumbled down the darkened passage after them, and fell over one of the sacks. A handful of spuds rolled along the floor and he scrabbled to pick them up. There were four one-hundredweight sacks.

That night he was so drunk he didn't remember getting to bed. He awoke at about four and lay for a couple of minutes, his head spinning sickly, wondering where he was and what the pain in his back could be. 'Himself' was snoring in the other bed like a buzz-saw, and in the long pauses between snores, Peter slowly became aware of other, lower snores, in various pitches, coming from the other rooms. Walls like paper, he thought. Oh God. The smell in the room was awful, a sweet reek of dirty clothes and sour beer fumes. He stumbled down the passageway to the lavatory, his bladder bursting. Should he pull the chain afterwards? Would he waken anybody? In the event he had to pull the chain first. The pan was full of vomit.

Next day Peter looked and felt like death. His headache was matched only by his backache. For the bed was broken, the springs completely without tension. They sagged like a bow, and his kidneys had actually been resting on the edge of his record player. In the university he was sick, and he couldn't face anything at lunchtime, neither food nor drink. Especially he couldn't face the Ducie. He wasn't going to let Kathleen see him in this state. At five o'clock he summoned up the courage to complain about the bed to Mrs O'Rourke, but her English seemed mysteriously to have left her, and his Irish was hardly good enough to have a fight in. She finally backed down to the extent of saying that Seamus O'Flaherty had a damn good bed, and when he left in a week or two he might have that. 'He's away back to Ireland,' she added, with an odd pride. 'He's done very well an' all. It's a damn fine bed, now.'

Tonight the food was mince. Boiled without salt, not

graced with a spot of anything else, and mostly lumps of fat and gristle. To garnish it – ho bloody ho, thought Peter – were a spoonful of cabbage mush and six large, soggy, boiled potatoes. There was a short conversation about a feller that had broke his leg falling off a plank, but it was mumbled through mouthfuls of spud so he only caught about a tenth of it. Then they were gone. Their drinking capacity was clearly fathomless, and equally clearly they did nothing else at all. There was no television in the house, no radio even that he ever saw, not a book nor a newspaper. The men apparently worked themselves half to death all day, and drank themselves half to death at night. Well, his professor had *said* there were other ways of learning Irish.

Peter went to the cinema that night, then took to his bed by ten thirty with four aspirin and a pint of milk inside him. He'd moved the record-player along, more under his feet, and he was so tired that even the huge sag in the mattress didn't keep him awake for long. Given the chance he'd have slept like a baby, till well into the morning. Given the chance.

Just before midnight he was awoken by an almighty crash. His bed was pushed sideways and jolted against the wall. Peter sat up in a panic, blinded by the electric light. On the old carpet, between the beds, lay 'Himself', flat on his back and groaning. One leg was bare and hairy, out of his trousers, the other still stuck fast inside. He was a weird colour in the face, a mixture of red and pale green. He opened his eyes and tried to focus on Peter, then gave up and closed them again. The leg that was half in the air slowly sank to the floor, and he began to snore: a horrible, bubbling sound, with enormous pauses in between. Outside in the passage there were a variety of other noises. A yelling, over and over again, of something Peter didn't understand, then a long snatch of quavering, sentimental singing. Over it came a woman's shout, thin and bitter: 'Call it off, will you, Mr Boyle, call it off I tell you,' followed by a stream of Gaelic. There were bangings as people fell against walls, a constant flushing of the lavatory, muffled curses. By twelve thirty the house was quiet again, except for the rumbling symphony of snores. And at six o'clock, he knew, the vans and trucks would arrive to take them to the cold roadworks, the freezing, frost-covered building-sites. He got out of bed, stepping carefully over the bubbling navvy on the floor, and switched the light out.

Peter lasted one more night before he abandoned his month's rent in advance, packed his stuff and went round to doss on Alan's floor till he could find another place. It wasn't being sat on at four thirty in the morning when 'Himself' tried to stagger upright to go and be sick, it wasn't the flea-bites he discovered later in the morning from his awful bed, it wasn't the third evening meal – although he didn't even manage one mouthful of the boiled liver that Mrs O'Rourke had concocted to go with the boiled cabbage and the pile of boiled praties. What clinched it was the midnight session.

He'd decided to stay in for the evening to do some work – and not before time. He couldn't, anyway, face the Ducie, still; it'd be too embarrassing. He'd asked, and got permission, to light a fire in the grate, and bought himself a litre bottle of Hirondelle and a takeaway Chinese that he'd smuggled upstairs under his coat. After he'd been reading and supping for a couple of hours he got a rosier glow on; he mellowed up. All right, so it was rough, rough as a bear's bum: but he could take it. They weren't such bad lads, just hard-drinking men. Once he'd got used to them and them to him he could start getting down to the Irish chat in earnest. He fell asleep about eleven o'clock feeling very Irish indeed. McTaggart, son of the priest. He giggled. It was good, that.

He woke briefly at around midnight to see 'Himself' hauling his clothes off, almost steady on his legs, turning off the light like a Christian, and creaking into bed. There was

72

the usual row outside, but Peter, wine-filled, drifted off again. He was having a good sexy dream about Liz, the girl he'd left in Hull, when it happened.

The door opened with a crash that almost took the wall out. Peter awoke with a jerk and half sat up. Silhouetted in the doorway, in the dull glow of the dying fire, was an enormous labourer, in longjohn underpants and a vest. He stood there swaying, his shoulders hitting the doorposts alternately. He was fumbling with the fly of his pants. There was a creak from the other bed as 'Himself' got up on one elbow, then the man staggered forward, just about keeping his balance. He stopped with a grunt as he reached the mantelpiece, and gave a long groan. Then, to Peter's total horror, there was a huge hiss and an explosion of sparks, steam and smoke. The room was filled with it, and the noise went on for minutes. When he had finished, the man half-turned, groaned once more, and fell sideways into the gap between the beds. Peter made a gagging noise, a croak of rage and shock. In the few seconds before the snores started, 'Himself' said mildly: 'Ah Christ, the dirty divvil. The poor sod's had a skinful, that's for sure.'

It was a week or more before he could bring himself to tell Kathleen he'd left, and why. Some of his outrage remained, and he said it had made him feel ashamed to be Irish. She clicked her tongue, half-sympathetically, as much as to question his right to say it, being third generation and all. Then she said: 'They're a bloody strange lot, Peter love, them from the bogs. Stout and spuds is what they lives on. It's all they got to cling to over here.' He looked at her, expecting more. She went on: 'I'd feel sorry for 'em, if I was you, love. I mean they're all alone like, in a foreign land. Have you ever thought of that? They've mostly got wives and children over there, you know, and they're sending back the money to give 'em a better life. Sure, England's the land of honey and milk to them. The streets is paved with gold. Only them's the ones that have to build the streets, no other buggers will. It'd be a damn long haul to get to Hull from here if the bogmen and the mountainy men hadn't made that old M62 for yez, I tell you that.'

Not more than a few days later, they were all in the snug telling Irish jokes. 'Did you hear about the Irishman who thought Salford Van Hire was a Dutch painter?' asked Kathleen. 'Isn't that just a bloody scream, that one!'

Peter said suddenly: 'How do you brainwash an Irishman?'

Everyone looked at him in surprise. It was the first time he'd ever told one, had ever joined in in any way on the jokes. Kathleen turned her eyes full on to him, quite slowly, and her face had lost its smile.

'You fill his wellies with water, Peter love,' she said. 'That's what they say.' She smiled once more, but it was only a small smile, full of sympathy and warning. 'But you're Irish yourself, you know. Don't forget it, Peter love, will you? You're young yet. Don't forget it, will you?'

She ruffled his hair as she went past to the bar.

'It's important,' she said. 'Very.'

The Common Good

IT WAS HOT in the Number One magistrates court, and after he'd got used to the strangeness of it all, Jim Barker found the whole thing rather boring. The prosecuting solicitor had been droning on for a good ten minutes, and Jim had heard it all a dozen times, of course. He'd never been in the dock before, but he'd been in the witness box – in the actual witness box in front of him and to the right – twice. Both times he'd been a witness for the prosecution, and both times the people in the dock had been found guilty, largely due to him. That was just another reason why he knew he had nothing to worry about. He was going to be acquitted.

He was going to be acquitted for lots of reasons, his solicitor, Mr Ellerman, had told him, and the main one was because he was innocent. As he listened to the prosecuting solicitor outlining what he called the 'facts' of the case, he began to get furious again. He was furious that he was there, standing in the dock in the Number One court, when he'd done nothing at all to deserve it. Mr Ellerman had talked to him a lot over the last few days, tried to make sure he'd be calm. But when he thought about it, when it came back to him, he felt the tightness in his chest, the rising fury. He'd done nothing, nothing at all, and he was up in front of the magistrates with his mum worried to death in the public gallery and that creep Peter Jackson, whom he'd known at school, sitting in the Press box scribbling it all down to plaster his name over the local paper if he got half a chance. It was ridiculous.

Jim tried to calm himself down by studying the big, packed, courtroom. Not for the first time his eyes wandered to the shorthand girl, who was taking it all down on a machine like a weird little typewriter. The last two times he'd been in the court the shorthand writer had been a bloke, a thin, weedy chap with an old-fashioned gingery suit on. This one was a real plus. She was terrific looking, pale-faced with long dark hair. Every now and then she lifted her fingers off the keys when the solicitor paused in his spiel and pushed it back out of her eyes. It was a habit, something to do with her hands; because obviously, she couldn't have worked if it had really been bothering her.

There was another woman behind her, but she was something else again. She was the chairman of the magistrates and she was an alderman too. But she was no run of the mill Tory lady, the sort of old dame that had made his Dad grind his teeth with rage just to see in the street when he'd been alive. She was youngish – in her early forties Jim guessed – and she was extremely good looking. She had on a pale camel suit that looked as if it had cost a million dollars, and she had an alive, alert, sort of face. She'd been the chairman on the last two times he'd been in the court, and she recognized him, he could tell. In fact he thought she'd given him just the ghost of a smile when he'd been brought in. He'd not dared to actually smile back, but it had given him a real boost, obviously. Every now and again, he'd seen her glancing at him, keen and not at all unfriendly. It was as if they were in league, in a funny sort of way. Anyway, it had to be another plus, because she knew the sort of bloke he was. She knew he wasn't a thug or anything, and that he'd been a star witness and got some villains sent down.

This cool-looking lady, Alderman Mrs Sotnick she was called, was flanked by two fellows of about ten years older. They were dressed in ordinary dark suits and he didn't know their names. But they were the usual run of magistrates, you could tell. They'd be accountants, or local builders, or newspaper editors or something. Respectable and boring, with kids that had gone to university and houses up the Avenue end. They were probably on the council, like her. It was funny, that. All the same sort of people seemed to do all the same sort of thing: magistrates, councillors, bosses. It wasn't right, when you thought about it. But he wasn't worried: Mrs Sotnick was there, and she was different. She'd see him right.

The prosecuting solicitor was standing in front of the high bench affair where the three magistrates were sitting, and he waved his arms about quite a bit as he talked. The sun shining through the high windows of the courtroom flashed on his pale grey suit and you could see he was enjoying himself. He looked a bit of a ponce on the quiet, Jim thought. He was a bit of a liar, certainly – a ruddy liar. But Jim had got his temper under control again. He didn't care. He listened to the 'facts' and some of them made him smile. Pure fiction, most of it. But he should worry. He was innocent.

'It was, your worships, just a further manifestation of the shameful events you have been forced to hear related in this courtroom so frequently in the past few days,' the prosecuting solicitor was saying. 'This young man, admittedly of previously good character, became involved in an attack upon the police and the forces of law and order that was outrageous, intolerable, and unprecedented in the history of this borough. You have heard it suggested many times that the circumstances made some sort of violent reaction likely, even inevitable. That this march, which led directly to the arrest of some three hundred people, should never have been allowed to take place. That the political organisation involved knew perfectly well that their presence would provoke anger among the local community, especially the Asian community. For the most part, this is not a

77

view to which you have allowed much credence, and I trust you will not in this particular case.'

He paused, running a finger through his already smooth black hair. His expression became more grave.

'The simple fact is, your worships,' he went on, 'that the violence, as you have heard time after time, was directed as much at the police as at the marchers, and was caused largely by large bodies of people who flooded this area from very widely scattered points *hell-bent* on causing trouble. This young man, although local, had as little justification as they. He quite deliberately, and with full awareness of what he was doing, indulged in behaviour that was quite likely to – and for all we know, before his apprehension in actual fact did – cause injury to an innocent policeman in the exercise of his duty. That duty, however much one may deplore the views of the marchers, was a sacred one: the upholding of the right of free speech. That fact, I suggest, should never be lost sight of.'

He folded the sheaf of papers in his right hand in two, and creased it abruptly with his left.

'That is all I wish to say in my opening remarks,' he said. 'The evidence you will hear will, I am certain, more than satisfy you of the prosecution's case. I would first call Police Sergeant Webster.'

Jim got a real shock of surprise when Sergeant Webster took the stand. For a start he wasn't in uniform. He was about forty, and very smartly dressed in a neat grey suit and a snowy white shirt. He had dark curly hair and a sort of friendly, pleasant face. For a moment Jim couldn't believe it was the same bloke. He had a sudden, crazy, notion that they'd put someone else in the witness box, someone pretending to be the sergeant. But that was daft. Even his voice was different, though; soft, and calm, and reasonable.

'I swear by Almighty God that the evidence that I give shall be the truth, the whole truth and nothing but the truth.'

It was absurd. Jim shivered. He remembered the sergeant's snarling, contorted face as he'd grabbed his arm and twisted it up his back until he'd screamed. He remembered the way, later, in the police station, he'd punched him in the stomach, and kicked him, and spat in his face. It was unbelievable.

The sergeant's evidence was brief, and to the point, and sounded utterly reasonable. On the day of the march, he said, he had been in command of a group of about thirty constables out of the total force of several hundreds. The area in which he had been controlling the crowds had been a particularly violent one, and several policemen had been injured, some of them seriously. The crowd, which had consisted mostly of Asians, with pockets of politically motivated whites, had been abusive and highly provocative. At first insults, then stones, sticks and bottles had been thrown. He had led several charges into the crowd, and made several arrests. On one of the charges he had seen the defendant, James Arthur Barker, holding a half-wallbrick which he clearly intended to throw at the police. His right arm was drawn back, his body was in a throwing stance, and he was shouting obscenities at the advancing officers. Yes, he could identify James Arthur Barker as the youth in the court; there. He was arrested and taken to Albert Road police station where he was formally cautioned, and charged with threatening behaviour and carrying an offensive weapon. At the police station he had been abusive, violent and had attempted to punch two police officers and kick another in the groin. A certain amount of force had had to be applied to bring him under control.

The sergeant looked round the court with a pleasant, honest look when he'd said his piece. Jim looked at his solicitor, Mr Ellerman, half expecting him to jump up and tear the story to pieces. Then he remembered. Mr Ellerman had said he wasn't going to cross-examine unless something was said that they weren't going to break down in their own evidence. He knew what he was doing, Jim was sure of that. He tried to relax, but he was shaken. It was incredible. It was a pack of lies, it was awful. Mr Ellerman indicated that he had no questions and the sergeant smiled and stepped down. As Jim looked up, so did the shorthand girl, and their eyes met. He felt a deep blush rise in his cheeks. He felt ashamed. What must she be thinking of him? It was awful.

The truth of the matter was, that Jim had had absolutely nothing at all to do with it. He'd had to go past the area where the demo was being held, because he had to go and order some parts from the continental spares shop down on Parkhill Road. The garage where he was an apprentice did a lot of foreign cars – you had to, nowadays – and he was always going down there for something or other. But he'd even forgotten about the demo, and the trouble, because he was more interested in cars than anything else, least of all politics. When his old man had been alive he'd tried to get him involved with Labour and all that, but Jim didn't give a tinker's curse, actually speaking. Nor for the Asians, either. There were a heck of a lot of them in this part of town, but they never bothered him at all, one way or the other. Take 'em or leave 'em alone, it was all one to him.

As he'd gone along Victoria Road he'd heard the row and he'd seen the edges of the crowd milling about in the side streets. It was a bright, warm day, and he wasn't in a particular hurry, so he'd sort of drifted down towards them to see what was what. And it had been fantastic. A bear garden, a real riot.

Jim only had a hazy idea of what was going on, but he soon realised it was pretty damn serious. He remembered the council had agreed to let the NF or some other fascist lot do a march, and he remembered his mum had got hot under the collar about it, although he hadn't been listening a lot to what she said. His mum still carried the banner for

Labour, like she'd done when the old feller was alive, and she reckoned it was a scandal that they could let a gang of racists march down streets where mainly Asians lived. She wasn't the only one, that was for certain. The roads were packed, solid, crammed, with people – black, white and khaki. There was a fantastic noise, a sort of rhythmic, roaring, growling sound. And behind it, every now and again, the two-tone blaring of police sirens, with occasionally that kind of whirring, whistling noise made by the new sirens, like on the American TV films.

Without meaning to, he'd got farther into the packed demonstrators than the very edge. The movements inside the crowds were like currents – you suddenly found yourself being moved along fast in one direction, held solid in a stream of bodies, your feet hardly touching the ground. It was quite frightening, in a way, but exhilarating with it. He moved his wallet out of his back pocket at one stage, and buttoned it into the front flap of his shirt. It would be a field day for pickpockets. Sometimes he found himself up towards the main road, where the march would be, and sometimes he'd be moved backwards. When the front of the procession actually came in sight, he was quite close to the kerb.

The weirdest thing about it all, was the rig-outs they wore. The marchers were carrying banners, with the usual crap racist slogans written on them, but they were mainly noticeable for the hunks of wood they were nailed to. They were thick, and heavy, with pointed tops or bits of metal bent over them. Jim was quite surprised, because they looked more like weapons to him. What's more, the fascists wore crash helmets, and dirty great boots, and tons of black leather gear. A lot of them looked terrified, pale-faced and spotty, but there were some big swines among them, enormous. Like apes, only not so good-looking.

Actually, the people apparently leading the march were the police. In front of the first batch there was a squad of

81

about forty of them, with plastic shields and anxious looks on their faces. There were more police lining the road, on both sides, hundreds of them, thousands maybe. And in the background the intermittent sirens, and the whirring sounds. Half the ruddy force must be here, Jim thought. Crazy idea, when you considered it. They seemed to be bent on protecting those half-wits, and meanwhile all the ruddy criminals for miles around must be thinking it's their birthdays!

It was while he was watching them, and thinking also how ridiculously young some of the coppers were, that the trouble started. Like everyone else, in the days that followed, he tried to work out exactly what had happened, but it was impossible ever to be sure. It was a monumental cock-up, that was the only certain thing, and it would have been a lot better for all concerned if it had never happened. But as to details ... no chance.

The first he knew that it was getting out of hand was the change in the note of the roaring noise. For no reason that he could see – although he guessed something must have happened farther down the road – the rhythmic, growling sound began to break up. There were sharper shouts, and bursts of yelling, then screams. Suddenly the air was full of screaming, and full of stones and bottles.

To Jim, crushed in the swaying mass, one of those peculiar things happened when time seems to go haywire. As he watched the leading batch of policemen, he could see a hail of missiles flying through the air towards them. But the missiles appeared to be suspended, hanging in the sky above their heads. Their faces changed in front of him, and it gave him a terrible shock. As they lifted their shields, protectively, the anxiety he'd noticed turned to fear. Not all of them, obviously, but some of them. As the chunks of glass and lumps of rock got closer, some of the faces whitened, tensed, contorted. Jim saw a jagged piece of paving stone smash into one of the shields, bounce off it, and crash into the cheek of a young policeman. He seemed even to hear his agonised wail as he dropped to one knee, with blood flowing down his cheek and through the fingers of the hand he put up to cover the wound. Time speeded up to normal again. The group of policemen covered their heads with their shields and the hail beat against them.

God, thought Jim, oh God, let me out of here. He didn't know why, but the fact of the policemen's fear shocked him deeply. It frightened him, it made him realise how desperate and dangerous the situation was. The whole thing was getting out of control; anything could happen. He twisted and turned violently to break free of the crowd. He started to force his way down the side street that led to Victoria Road. He wouldn't have got clear, but the front ranks of the mob where he was trapped began to break up as the noise got louder and more confused.

He started pushing harder, and all round him people were doing the same, trying to get away. As they ran *from* the scene of the action, people at the back surged forward *to* it. They began to shout at each other, to scream and punch, as the rocks and bottles rained down. Every now and then Jim caught a glimpse of blue, and saw truncheons beating up and down on the crowd. He was terrified, he was damn nearly gibbering with fright. Then, to his immense relief, he burst out of the edge of the crowd, like a cork from a champagne bottle. He was clear!

As Jim started to run like hell for Victoria Road, about ten policemen burst out of a side alley and raced towards him. He dodged to one side, beside a parked ambulance, to let them get past. Good luck to you, mates, he thought. Rather you than me! I wouldn't be in your shoes for a thousand pounds a week, dealing with that lot! It was then he saw the contorted face of Sergeant Webster. It was about all he saw. He was smashed to the ground, kicked in the stomach and the head, then hauled to his feet with his arm so far up his back that he thought he was going to faint, except he was screaming so hard. Later, in the Albert Road copshop, he was shown the wallbrick he was meant to have been flinging, and smacked about and kicked a bit, and called an effing Paki-lover. He was charged the next morning, having admitted absolutely nothing.

By the time he'd listened to four police constables, three of them with beards and all of them with looks of pure good-natured honesty on their faces, tell exactly the same story as Sergeant Webster had done, Jim had got his cool back. He was an easy-going sort of guy, and he'd never had anything against coppers as a breed like some of his mates had. There was a West Indian fitter he'd once worked with called – typically – Winston Spencer Jefferies, who'd insisted on referring to them as pigs, and Jim had always said (apart from it takes one to know one, which led to friendly punch-ups) that if you insisted on calling people names like that you could hardly complain if they cut up rough. Now he was shaken more than somewhat.

But he'd got his cool back. The only venom left in him was imagining what would happen to this lot when they were shown up to be the slimy, corrupt, lying, swine that they were. He allowed himself half a smile, of anticipation. He hoped they'd be kicked out of the force, and then jailed for perjury. And he hoped the other cons would kick seven kinds of crap out of them for having been coppers in the first place.

The last policeman to give evidence was the first one Mr Ellerman cross-examined.

'Can you tell the court please, Constable, which hand the defendant used to throw the house-brick?'

'I did not say he threw it, sir. I said he was about to throw it.'

'I beg your pardon. I am glad to see you are so concerned to be accurate. With which hand, then, was he *about* to throw it, if you please?'

The policeman looked a trifle put out, but there wasn't

much he could do about it as he'd already said it in evidence.

'The right hand, I believe, sir,' he said.

'You "believe", Constable? Are you not sure?'

'I ... I believe I am sure, sir.'

'Good,' said Mr Ellerman. 'That at least agrees with the evidence given by your colleagues. I thank you for your accuracy ... and consistency.'

The policeman smiled, relieved.

'Thank you, sir,' he said.

Mr Ellerman smiled back.

'You are aware I am sure, Constable,' he said icily, 'that my client is left-handed?'

There was a definite silence in the court. Outside Jim heard a motor-bike accelerate away. It sounded like a Norton. Too noisy for a Jap. He grinned to himself. That'll show you, you pig, he thought.

The policeman started: 'I ...' But Mr Ellerman turned away.

'That is all, Constable,' he said. 'I thank you.'

Although he didn't believe in religion, Jim had been told by Mr Ellerman that it was a big mistake to 'affirm', as it was called, rather than take the oath. If you lied on the Bible, he said, magistrates believed you. If you told the truth as an atheist, they didn't. He put his hand on the Bible that the usher held and said solemnly: 'I swear by Almighty God that the evidence that I give shall be the truth, the whole truth, and nothing but the truth.' It ruddy well will be, too, he added to himself. Which is more than any we've heard so far today. On an impulse, he looked up at Alderman Mrs Sotnick; an earnest, anxious look. He wanted it to tell her just how honest he was, and he wanted her to respond. She couldn't, of course, that was daft. But she met his eyes and she did not try to look away. Her gaze was level and unflustered, her eyes calm and grey. It was Jim who looked away, but he was strangely reassured. It was as if they understood each other. She was all right, and she knew. He was tremendously reassured.

'Are you James Arthur Barker?'

'Yes, sir.'

'And you are eighteen years old, an engineering apprentice?'

'Fitter mechanic, sir, yes, sir.'

'And you live at 15, Sebastopol Terrace in this borough?'

'Yes, sir.'

At first as he told his story, Jim stumbled and got confused. But he relaxed after a while, and it all came out pretty well. He admitted, in cross-examination, that he had sworn at the police in Albert Road police station, but said it was only after he had been spat at. Examined by his own solicitor he revealed that he had on two occasions in the last eight months reported incidents to the police, and that on both occasions they had secured criminal convictions. In the second case, he agreed, the defendants, who had been found guilty of attempting to steal a light van, had been Asians. He thought this line of questioning was rather unpleasant, but he saw what Ellerman was getting at: if the police wanted to paint him as fanatically pro-black, they'd picked the wrong sucker. He agreed that he'd had nothing to do with the demo, didn't know anyone taking part, and had been an innocent bystander trying to get out of a difficult situation when he'd been attacked and beaten by the police.

As the defence witnesses told their stories one by one, the whole business of why he'd ever ended up in court came back to him very strongly. The heat of the afternoon and the sleepy buzz of voices no longer made him feel bored and tired, he was fascinated. A dentist who'd been passing the end of the street said quite clearly that Jim had been running away when he'd been set on and beaten up, and further that he had quite definitely not been carrying a weapon of any sort, let alone a half wallbrick. I am, the dentist added, a member and former president of the local Round Table, and hardly given to telling lies.

Then not one but two of the ambulancemen who'd been nearby said he'd been deliberately attacked by the police, and one of them added that Sergeant Webster had appeared to be 'quite hysterical'. His family doctor confirmed that he was left-handed, and said that he had examined him the day after the march and found cuts, bruises and swellings which in his opinion could most easily have been received during the course of a moderately severe beating. Finally there were three character witnesses who said he was quiet, respectable, law-abiding and a thoroughly decent citizen.

Jim felt a right jerk. But he also felt pretty damn confident. He was almost surprised that Alderman Mrs Sotnick didn't tell him he wasn't guilty there and then, and apologise into the bargain. But when it was all over the three magistrates put their heads together for a few seconds and said they were going out to consider their verdict. Jim moved around to stretch his legs. He had backache and his bottom hurt. Mr Ellerman came towards him with a smile.

'Well, Jim,' he said. 'All over bar the shouting. I shouldn't think they'd be long.'

'Do you think . . . do you . . . I mean?'

Mr Ellerman smiled.

'You just relax,' he said. 'Remember what I told you yesterday. We won't talk about it now, just relax. And try not to worry.'

Jim looked at the high, panelled ceiling of the room. In the last few days, in this court, about six dozen demonstrators had been tried, found guilty, and fined. Some of them had even been sent to jail. In almost every case, he knew, the evidence against them had been so feeble as to be practically unbelievable. He'd talked it over in Mr Ellerman's office. He'd been terrified.

'Yes,' Mr Ellerman had said yesterday. 'I must admit I've been shaken myself, Jim. But I don't think we have much to worry about. Our witnesses are impeccable. I'd be absolutely astonished if you were to be convicted, sincerely I would. Astonished.'

'But look at that case on Monday,' said Jim. 'I mean, that kid was actually hoicked out of an ambulance by the police. Then they said he was heaving rocks! It's ruddy—'

'Jim,' Mr Ellerman had interrupted. 'Among other things, that kid has put the ambulancemen against the police. For us, that's an advantage, agreed? Another thing is that he was Asian; and unemployed, to boot. Think about it.'

Jim thought about it.

'That march,' Mr Ellerman went on, 'was a disaster. It was a ridiculous, awful, mistake. Not to mince matters, I believe the police over-reacted to say the least of it, although that's not to say they were entirely to blame. There must have been five thousand people trying to get at the marchers, and it was the duty of the police to protect them, right or wrong. Missiles were hurled, insults were passed, the provocation was intolerable. Some of them, as you yourself noticed, almost certainly acted out of sheer terror. If anybody was to blame, it was the authorities. The people sitting on the magistrates' bench, Jim, represent the authorities. They are unlikely to admit any fault. That is not authority's way.'

Jim thought about that, too.

'But you said I'd get off. If the magistrates are the authorities . . . I mean, I don't see why the fact I'm white should . . .'

Mr Ellerman had smiled.

'Look,' he'd said. 'I can't explain it easily. It's very difficult. Magistrates represent authority, and so do the police. The magistrates – almost certainly without knowing it – are biased in favour of the police. If it were their word

88

against yours, they would win. No contest. But it's not. Our witnesses are impeccable, and they're respectable. The police say they saw you threatening to hurl a half wallbrick, our witnesses say you were not. The fact that you're white and not Asian is as important as the fact that you're an apprentice and not unemployed. In this borough, in general, Asians in court mean problems: language difficulties, religions, customs, that sort of thing. Hard work and frustration. In this series of cases they represent trouble — way over two hundred black arrests, remember. And to most magistrates, unemployed equals layabout.'

'Jesus.'

'Yes,' Mr Ellerman had said dryly. 'It would take him to sort this mess out fairly. But I don't think we need worry. Even if the magistrates think it's necessary to accept absolutely what the police say in most of these cases, just for the general good, to make people respect the law, I don't think they will here. Our case is too strong. Apart from anything else, we *know* you're innocent. You'll see.'

Everyone stood up when the magistrates returned, and Jim remained standing. Alderman Mrs Sotnick shuffled the papers in front of her and looked at him. Again her grey eyes were calm and unflinching, and he knew immediately it was all right. Despite himself he felt a small smile begin to form. Mrs Sotnick looked down. She cleared her throat and began.

'James Arthur Barker,' she said, in her pleasant, well-modulated voice, 'my colleagues and I have found this a most difficult case to try. We have given the evidence an enormous amount of thought, and we have taken into account your previously excellent relationships with the police and your current character as related to us by witnesses. Although it would of course be improper for us to consider in conjunction with this case the others we have heard arising from the same series of events, it has equally been quite impossible not to make certain comparisons and find certain patterns of behaviour. Because of these patterns we have decided, albeit with some reluctance, to find you guilty on both counts.'

The pit of Jim's stomach dropped away to nothing with amazing suddenness. He stared at the pleasant, open face with utter amazement. He just could not believe it. It was several seconds before his mind caught up with Mrs Sotnick's voice once more.

'... truth from untruth,' she was saying. 'But one thing that has emerged with increasing clarity is this. You, like everybody else who was in the vicinity, must have been there for a reason. While in your case we are quite satisfied that you meant well – at least to begin with – the fact remains that it ended in disaster. This sort of behaviour, for whatever motive, is not now, never has been, nor ever can be for the good of the community, white or Asian.'

His mind slipped off again, this time in fury. Good of the community! Good of the community! Sod the community! He didn't give a damn for it, that had been his old man's thing, that's what his mum was always on about. He hadn't even remembered about the march, it was insane. He was an innocent bystander! He was a passer-by!

Alderman Mrs Sotnick had raised her head to stare at him. He was aware of his hands, gripping the dock rail. He forced himself to calm down, to breathe more slowly. He felt terribly shaky.

'In the past few days,' she said, 'it has become increasingly apparent, also, that it is all too easy to undermine the rule of law. Our police, who on this occasion were doing an almost impossible job, suffered a great number of injuries, many of them severe. While the injuries to members of the public received an enormous amount of attention in the Press, however, these injuries went almost unreported. To the journalistic mind, clearly, photographs of policemen reacting to acts of almost bestial provocation are much more "newsworthy". There is no doubt at all in our minds

90

that many of the people involved in this demonstration came into the borough, from outside, to quite deliberately cause trouble to further political ends. Many of them have since sought, by telling extravagant tales of so-called brutality, to bring the police force into disrepute. They are a vulnerable target.'

Oh oh oh, Mr Ellerman, Jim thought! So this is what you meant by bias! So this is what law and order's all about! He looked at Sergeant Webster, looked round at him at the back of the court, with his four chums. They gazed ahead, blank and bland. Five policemen, and all of them bent as nine-bob notes, he thought. And this gang of ratbags believed them. Oh oh oh!

'Finally, James Arthur Barker,' said Alderman Mrs Sotnick, 'we wish to make it clear that this court is in no way a party to prejudice of any kind. This too has been suggested in the Press, and is an attitude that we will show to be false. Many of the defendants in the preceding days have been, through no fault of their own, unfamiliar with the rules of custom and fair play that are – and, we are determined, shall remain – part and parcel of the British way of life. For you, that is not so. You have not their excuse. And the severity of the sentences we are going to pass on you will reflect that advantage in understanding that you chose to disregard.'

She paused, and her eyes seemed to bore into him.

'The only prejudice to be found in this court,' she said, 'is directed in favour of the rule of law and against all those who wish to damage it. Against criminals, thugs and hooligans. And we are not ashamed to name that prejudice, nor to exercise it. Is there anything you wish to say?'

Even if he'd had anything to say, Jim could not have spoken. He was still gripping the rail, stunned and trembling. He looked at the pretty shorthand girl, her fingers still, hovering over the keys, waiting for him to speak. He almost let out an enormous sob. Oh Mrs Sotnick, with your honest grey eyes! They didn't believe him, or they believed in law and order more. Oh Mrs Sotnick! He shook his head, violently, blinking back tears of rage and shame.

When he left the courtroom five minutes later, he owed the State two hundred pounds in fines and eighty pounds in costs. And not much in respect any more. Very little indeed.

A Sense of Shame

ALTHOUGH ALL THE LADS in the printing works reckoned she was one of the fittest bits they'd ever seen, the strange fact about Lorraine was she'd never been in love. She was quite tall, and put together very nicely thank you, and she had this long blonde hair that some claimed she'd said she could sit on if she had no clothes on – and many a fantasy *that* had led to when the inky-finger apprentices lay in their baths of a night. But until the time she took up with Mohammed, she had quite definitely never been in love.

She wasn't a prude, or anything like that, though. When she'd been at Highmoor Comprehensive she'd been out with quite a lot of the older lads, and she wasn't averse to a bit of kissing in the pictures or at the back of a disco. Nothing more than kissing, true, but even now she was only sixteen. She earned peanuts at old Crawthorpe's printing works, but if anyone suggested she ought to get her kecks off and put her frozen assets into business to make *real* money – on Page Three of the *Sun* for instance – she'd either choke them off or giggle, depending on who said it. She didn't take it seriously, anyway. She knew she wasn't *that* special. Her hair was awful if she didn't wash it every two days and she had her fair share of spots like everybody else. Steve, the oldest apprentice, was the only one who'd taken her out from work, and he'd made a right berk of himself. He'd borrowed his brother's car – a dead smart Vauxhall estate with the reclining seats and all – and after a Chinkie meal in the middle of Manchester he'd taken her for a drive over the moors above Oldham, where they lived and where the printing works was. Quite a nice time they had too, he reckoned. They buzzed around and had a drink at one of those poncy moorland pubs and it was all looking very promising. Then he pulled the oldest stunt of all – he pretended to run out of petrol. She was out of the car so fast he didn't see her for dust, just storming off down Rippon-den Road as if she was prepared to walk all the way to the town centre if a bus didn't show up. Steve, it must be admitted, played the gent and went after her. But it certainly ruined his prospects.

Lorraine met Mohammed by one of those chances that happen at work. She'd been the office junior for some time, and after a while, because her typing didn't get much better and her spelling was terrible, old Crawthorpe had asked her if she could add up. He put on a real act of surprise when she said she could, and really was surprised when he gave her some simple money sums to do and she whipped through in a couple of minutes and got them right. Lorraine didn't mind Crawthorpe, although he was a crusty old devil, so she didn't get on her high horse. She smiled and said: 'I weren't that good at much at Highmoor, Mr Craw-thorpe, but I were right good at maths.' When she'd been in the accounts department for a mere two weeks, in walked Mohammed.

She was sixteen, he was nineteen. She was white Oldham and a Catholic too (although the days when the Catholics in Oldham got the nasty end of the prejudice stick are long gone) and he was a Pakistani. She was tall, blonde and good-looking, and dressed in a pair of dead tight jeans and a white mohair sweater. He was dressed in a set of overalls, a boiler-suit affair, covered in black ink. He too was tall, very tall. He was dark brown, even for a Pakistani, had jet black hair, and brilliant, piercing, enormous brown eyes. Lorraine's knees turned to jelly. She'd never felt anything like it. She turned away. She *fancied* him.

'Eh, love,' he said, Oldham through and through. 'Is boss in? I've finished that job. Is there owt else or am I to get back to th'works?'

When he'd gone, a few minutes later, even old Crawthorpe noticed she was in a state.

'What's up, lass?' he asked gruffly. 'Are you not reight? It weren't that Paki, were it? He didn't say owt? You look reight upset.'

Lorraine sat down with a bump. She'd often fancied boys before, or so she thought, but she'd never felt this, ever. She'd read about love at first sight often enough, in the magazines, and half believed it could happen – to others. But to her? With a Pakistani! It was ridiculous, nuts. She had nothing against them, but well! Everyone said she was a cracker. She was certainly all right. And one day, she'd always known, one day she'd meet somebody fantastic. But a Paki! She felt right weird. It was ridiculous.

'No, Mr Crawthorpe,' she got out at last. 'Course not. No. Just a bit . . . I've just kind of lost me breath a minute.'

'I'll put kettle on,' he said kindly. 'We'll have a cup of instant.' He bustled about, filling the electric kettle at the big white sink. 'Ruddy Pakis get everywhere, don't they, lass? I thought he might've said summat. He's a darn good worker, that one. Works for Pritties. Every time owt goes with one of presses I ask for 'im by name. Red 'ot he is.' He laughed. 'Well, not by name, exactly, but you know what I mean! Yon black beggar, I say. Old Man Pritty allus gives a chuckle. But he's a reight good little worker.'

Life in Crawthorpe's printing works, for Lorraine, was one big drag. She sat in a small office, more a large box, with walls made of plasterboard and sheafs of invoices hanging from them on bulldog clips, at a large untidy table with a calculator and pads of printed forms to record all the money going in and out of the firm. In a corner was the sink, with a draining board and kettle, next to that was the door to the lavatory that she and the girls from the other office, the one she'd been kicked out of, shared, and next to that the door to old Crawthorpe's office, that he called the Inner Sanctum. Opposite her was the half-glassed door to the printing shed, where the constant clacking and hissing came from and the inky boys poked their heads in every now and again to chat her up. Customers came in through it as well, and anyone else who wanted the boss. Before Mohammed, it had been her one source of interest, wondering who might come in, for like most office girls she didn't have a lot to do, not enough to keep her occupied. She was paid peanuts and she more than earned them, just for suffering the grinding dragginess of it all. Now, it became more than a source of interest. Try as she might to pretend nothing had happened, try as she might to push the unwanted thoughts out of her mind, the door became the focal point of her life.

It was crazy. Before, when she hadn't had an account to do up, or an invoice to sort out, she'd just mooned about, bored but not particularly miserable, rather like her last years in school. She'd read the true romance picture mags that the girls bought on a pool system, she'd done her nails or gone into the cloakroom and tried different ways with her hair, she'd thought about whether to go to the holiday camp at Scarborough with her friend Jackie or whether they should try for Majorca this year – wondered whether they'd dare when it came down to it, two young girls on their own. Wondered, for that matter, whether her dad would let her; he was a right old-fashioned get over things like that. All in all she'd just passed her time dreaming vaguely about things that didn't matter much. She'd been in a sort of limbo.

Now she was totally changed. She was obsessed. She was a horrible mixture of wanting and worry. She watched the half-glassed door like a hawk, willing it to open and

Mohammed to come in – not that she knew his name, of course. Every time it opened and it *wasn't* him she felt a lurch of disappointment, that sometimes bordered on anger at the person who'd come into the office. She got snappy and anxious. And when Jackie noticed it and asked her why, she nearly chewed her head off. It was crazy, she knew it was crazy, and she fought it as hard as she could. Some days she thought she was winning, some mornings she woke up and her mind was free of him, blank, calm. But during the day, always, she'd realise that she'd stopped work, stopped concentrating, stopped doing anything but think of him. And watch the door. She knew somehow that if she could hold out long enough this whole stupid thing would go away, would just fade and disappear. But she wanted to see him. She desperately wanted to see him.

Lorraine had never worried much about Pakistanis before. The part of Oldham she'd lived in since a baby was full of Poles and Ukrainians who'd come in because of the war, who still kept their own language and customs, and nobody bothered. Her being a Catholic helped, and all – she knew that when her dad and mum had first moved in the Irish had had a lot of trouble, window-smashing and not getting jobs and being hated and such, and that had passed away in the end. Then as the town gradually got its blacks, and Pakistanis and Bengalis, you got used to 'em and they certainly never troubled her. There was the odd outburst, naturally, and the National Front nazis got up to their pathetic tricks from time to time, but her dad had fought in the war, and been to Germany in 1945, and the very mention of racialism made him froth at the mouth with rage. He'd seen the camps. When the NF candidate in the local election had come knocking on their door one night he'd almost got his teeth smashed down his throat.

But going out with one, even thinking of it. That was different. Lorraine had this hollow, hopeless feeling. When she went to the clubs with Jackie, or when she was walking round the streets or in Tommyfields market, she found herself looking at them. She'd catch herself out, eyeing up the young lads, wondering at the grease in their black hair, wondering at their leanness and how poor most of them looked, wondering at their cheap thin shoes. The way they talked among themselves in a foreign language, then spoke to customers – those with textile stalls – in Oldham accents, some of them, fascinated her and repelled her. On the X-12 single-decker one day, the bus that went from Manchester to Bradford through Oldham and was always three-quarters full of Pakistanis, she heard a driver being rude to an old guy in one of those funny hats they wore, who spoke practically no English at all, and she got terribly upset. But confused with it. She didn't know whose side she was on, didn't know who she liked or hated. And the idea of fancying one! My God, what did it mean? Much as her father hated racism, she couldn't begin to imagine what he'd say to that as an idea! She knew right well that in his book she would even have to *marry* a Catholic, never mind it being the nineteen-eighties! And she'd look at a Pakistani in the street and think: I don't, it's all right, I *don't* fancy them. Of course he's not special, he's just a boy. A tall, thin, Pakistani boy. Fancy him! I must've been mad! And she'd find herself sitting at work staring at the half-glassed door, find her nails biting into her palms with tension as she listened to the steady clack and hiss of the presses, *willing* one to go funny, to break down. Anything so this tall, thin, unfancied boy would come back through that door.

When he did at last, Lorraine truly nearly fainted. She was standing, putting a bunch of invoices under a bulldog clip, when the handle went, and she turned – she was keyed up like a fiddle string – saw who it was, and did a half-lurch to her seat. She tore the leg of her tights on the corner of a drawer and sat down gasping, red and foolish. He looked worried for a moment, then smiled. 'You aw reight, lass?' he said. 'You look like you've been running. Has th'owd

98

feller been chasing you round desk?' Lorraine tried to smile back, but it wobbled. When he'd gone into the inner sanctum she pushed her legs right under the kneehole of the desk so that he wouldn't see her torn tights and tried to pull herself together. She was trembling and she felt sick. She'd never been so happy in her life, nor so miserable. She wanted to die.

Mr Crawthorpe saw Mohammed out of the office, because he remembered how queer Lorraine had got last time. Lorraine had her head down, studying something furiously on the blotter in front of her. When the door closed old Crawthorpe looked at her, said, 'Aw reight, lass?' decided she was, and disappeared into his room. Lorraine let out a long, shuddering sigh. A wave of misery that she'd never known before swept over her. She felt drowned. She couldn't stand it any more. Not more weeks of this. Not more weeks of staring at that *bloody* door.

The door opened and Mohammed peeped in to see if it was clear. A tension like a charge of electricity filled the room. Lorraine stared at him, and although she knew her mouth was open she couldn't close it. His face was tense, worried, his voice unsure, in case he was making a terrible mistake.

'Would you . . . could I . . . like, give you a lift home, like?' he said. 'You know, after work?'

His head hovered in the doorway full of anxiety, ready to disappear at the first, tiniest sign of a sneer. Lorraine said: 'Yuh.' It was all she could get out. A smile burst over his dark face, his eyes glowed. 'Great!' he said, softly. 'Where will I meet you? I've got a spare helmet.'

'Away,' stuttered Lorraine. 'By . . . by . . . Higsons, the chemists. D'you know it?' It had to be away. She couldn't meet him nearer. Well away, well away.

'Yeah,' he said. 'Five thirty?'

She nodded dumbly, filled with happiness, shame and terror. If old Crawthorpe only opened that door! She jerked her head backwards to indicate it and Mohammed nodded.

'Eh,' he said, looking daftly happy. 'Eh, thanks lass.'

The next couple of months were the happiest Lorraine had ever had in her life. A couple of times, lying alone under her pink quilt in the little brick house she shared with her parents and her small brother Frederick, she had a cold, quick feeling, that it was the happiest time she was ever likely to. But the icy clutch at the pit of her stomach passed away almost immediately. She'd lie there, in a glow of love, remembering the joys of the evening, half aware of the sound of the TV downstairs and the cars away over on the main road, and waiting for tomorrow to come, for work to pass, and for Mohammed to be waiting, sitting astride his lovely Honda in whichever secret spot in the town-centre bustle they'd chosen to meet.

The very first evening, they'd met formally of course, and they'd kept that up ever since, by an unspoken agreement. Mohammed would wait until he saw her moving along the street, then he'd get off and stand beside the bike with her crash-helmet already unbuckled. They'd say hello, almost like strangers, and she'd bundle up her long blonde hair and pull the huge, red spaceman helmet down to cover it. The first time she'd done it naturally, not knowing whether to leave it flying free or not, but it occurred to her almost immediately that it made her chances of being not recognised much better. She felt vaguely shamed by the thought, but she kept up the deed. Mohammed always wore a scarf across the lower part of his face, so that he didn't look like a Pakistani at all, unless you peered close. She never asked him why. But when they got outside the town, sometimes, in the warm wind, she'd let her hair fly out behind, like a beautiful long blonde flag. And Mohammed would unmask his face, folding up the tartan scarf and putting it in the pocket of his leather jacket. That first night they hadn't kissed, they *had* been strangers. But afterwards, when they'd said hello, and Lorraine had got her crash-hat on, they would drive somewhere quickly, not far but to where they would not be known, then stop the bike and fling their arms round each other as if their lives depended on it, and kiss and kiss, and squeeze the love from each of their bodies into the other. Lorraine almost always fell asleep dreaming about that, and woke with longing.

The first night was formal, and although it was a warm night in the spring, they could think of nothing else to do but go to a cafe. They went to the Precinct, right in the middle, because nobody went there, it was a huge, hideous, empty dump that the council were so ashamed of they'd gone and built another one nearby, to prove they'd not made a mistake. They stuck the bike round the back and sat in a corner of a tea-room drinking coffee and eating cakes. There weren't many other people in and no one took any notice of them, but Lorraine was in a fine old state. Every time she lifted her cup off her saucer it rattled, and she kept her mouth full as much of the time as she could. She kept thinking she must be mad, sitting supping coffee with a Pakistani she didn't even know. But then she'd catch him looking at her, and herself looking at him, and an enormous smile of pure, crazy happiness spread over both their faces and her blood would race and she'd feel quite dizzy. She dropped her spoon once and they both reached at the same moment and their heads banged together beside the table and they left them there, touching. He whispered: 'My name's Mohammed. What's yours?'

When they got round to talking, they talked about nothing at all. Did she like motorbikes? Wasn't the weather nice? How long had she worked at Crawthorpe's? All that sort of nonsense. What schools they'd been to, what films they'd seen, where they went drinking, whose records they liked, did they know so-and-so? There were no pauses, none at all, they talked like they'd known each other for ages. But they didn't *say* anything. Lorraine's eyes flicked constantly between the coffee pattern she was drawing on the table with her spoon, and his face. He had a thin face, with a little black 'tache and high cheekbones. His eyes were enormous, brown and liquid. He was wearing a sports jacket, now he'd taken his leather off, with his shirt collar outside like Pakistanis did, and a pair of good jeans. To her he was fantastic.

She could have stayed all evening, would have done if it had been up to her. But she suddenly realised she was late for her tea, and her Mum would be worried, and she had a date with Jackie to go to the Hole in the Wall. Mohammed said he was booked up, too, and they both of them got jealous. Well not jealous, exactly, but worried. She said lightly, but her voice almost wavering: 'I s'pose you've got a date?' He didn't laugh. 'No, I've got to see my mate,' he replied. 'We're in business. Well. We're working on a car. It *is* a business. I'll tell you. Why – are you meeting with a bloke, like?' He said it not as if to say 'it's nothing to me, go ahead', he said it as if to say 'I hope you're not. I wish you wouldn't. I want it to be me.' 'No,' said Lorraine, 'I'm not. I'm meeting Jackie. She's my mate. We're going down the Hole.' 'Dancing?' 'Aye, well. I s'pose so. Not jealous are you?' He looked at her with his liquid eyes, half-serious, half-mocking. 'I might be,' he said at last. 'Am I to see you again?' It never entered her head to play hard to get. She answered: 'If you like. I could ... I could ... Tomorrow. After work. We could go a drive. If you like. I like motor-bikes, me.' They stared at each other across the table, half scared. 'Yeah,' he said.

Sometimes the weather does the wrong things, sometimes it seems to know exactly what's going on and do its best to help. From their first trip across the moors together, for week after week, what in the end felt like month after month, it did nothing to stand in their way. They got into a pattern that grew so strong that it matched their love and somehow reflected it. They'd meet, formally always, after work, and drive away and kiss and sometimes have a coffee.

102

Then they'd both go off home and have their teas. Then Lorraine would go out again – always, if her parents asked, to meet Jackie or the other Catholic girls her father had no qualms about at all – and race to the spot where Mohammed had arranged to meet her. They'd kiss, again and always as if they wanted to absorb each other, become one person, then they'd head off to the moors.

Lorraine had lived in Oldham all her life, but she'd never realised, till she fell in love, just what lay outside it. She'd always seen the mountains – the town lies almost in a bowl of them, except the Manchester side – but she'd never bothered with them. But Mohammed had, and over the weeks he took her by all the routes out of town that led them to the moors. They went up the Ripponden Road through Grains Bar and Denshaw to the bleak heights where you could count over three hundred mill chimneys on the plain, they took the A62 over Scouthead, through Delph to Stanedge and the long drop into Marsden and Huddersfield, they took the fabulous Isle of Skye road up to the heights over Dovestones and across to Holmfirth. They'd drive for hours, not fast, exploring all the small roads and the bye-ways and the little towns and villages, with Lorraine's long hair blowing out in the westering sun which glinted off the brown angles of Mohammed's face. Sometimes they parked the bike in the shade of a stone wall and wandered down to one of the reservoirs that dotted the area, or climbed to a high, windy peak. Sometimes they had a drink in a little lonely pub they'd found. Always they talked, except when they were doing a fast run for the hell of it on a good bit of mountain road. Always they talked.

Mohammed, it turned out, had come to England at an early age, four or five he thought, with his father and two older brothers. All three of them worked in textiles, on night shifts in one of the big combine mills, and because they were older when they'd come in they didn't speak the language as well as he did. They were a lot more old-fashioned, too, in matters of religion and such, and he often got into trouble with his brothers, who reckoned he should do more of what they told him and less of what he fancied. But he'd learned the language fast, got on well at school, and had got an apprenticeship with Pritties, the printing trades engineers. He also had a white mate called Bill, who owned a small garage, and this caused trouble with his family. He was doing a sort of unofficial training with Bill, who was a lot older than he was, and they were hoping to get a real business going, renovating cars, especially old ones, that they could get dead cheap as almost wrecks and sell for a damn good price.

'I'm a natural, see,' he said, as they sat in the sun outside a moorland pub one evening. 'Bill reckons I've got a real feel for engines, I'm not bragging, he'll let me strip down anything. He's – we've – not got a lot of capital yet, but he reckons we're almost ready to talk to a bank, set up a small factory, like. Honest, Lorraine, if we can get that started, the sky's the flaming limit. Honest.'

She was happy to stare into his shining eyes, watch his neck muscles move as he swallowed his beer. Lorraine felt sorry, now, that she'd learned so little at school. She sometimes got bitter with her teachers for letting her stay so ignorant, and with herself for not having the nouse to realise. She knew nowt, damn all, and Mohammed knew so much. His factory seemed like a dream, right enough, but she knew he'd do it, she knew they'd get it off the ground. She was useless.

'When it's started, though,' she said. 'When you and Bill've got it going, like, you'll need a girl. I mean, to do the money and that. You'll need a girl to do your VAT.'

'Eh, kid, fantastic!' said Mohammed in delight. 'You can come in too! We'll all work together! Eh, that's a great plan, lass! Great!'

They never mentioned Mohammed's brothers' disapproval of his white friend Bill and what that meant they'd think of her. They never mentioned what her Dad would say if he knew she was going with a Paki. They never mentioned the future. And when Lorraine caught herself dreaming, in the slack times at the office, say, or in her bed, dreaming the normal, ordinary dreams she'd always had, like marriage, and honeymoons and that, she jerked her mind away to other things, just wouldn't think about it.

Two nights a week, regular as clockwork, come hell or highwater, Mohammed went round to the workshop to help Bill do up the latest 'product' as they called it. And Lorraine, because she wanted to and because she felt bad about it anyway, went out with Jackie. At first, she'd made up lies about why she was never on the town anymore – before Mohammed they'd gone out almost every night – even going so far as to say once that she'd started going to night school. She didn't quite know why, but it had to be this way. She had imaginary conversations, when she told her friend the truth, and they always ended up the same. Somehow or other, using words or not, Jackie told her how she felt: it was a mistake, a terrible mistake. Lorraine and a Pakistani. It was such a waste. She'd chucked herself away. Jackie, who'd been her best friend for long enough, didn't call her a liar outright, and didn't even get very hurt. She knew damn well that Lorraine had a feller, and also that the time would come when she'd get told. The fact that she was in love stuck out a mile: even the blokes at work made remarks about her looking like she was getting enough for three. What Jackie couldn't understand was the secrecy.

One night when they'd been to a club, and Lorraine, as usual these days, had hardly danced with anyone, they left early. Lorraine had suggested it, and Jackie didn't care either way – it wasn't a bag of laughs sitting with a self-imposed wallflower. They decided to walk home, because it was the middle of summer, and the air was clean and warm. Lorraine noticed the mountains nowadays, not ignored them like she had in the past. She sighed as she looked at the long winding strings of orange lights disappearing up into the velvet sky.

'Crikey, Lorraine,' said Jackie. 'You sound like a sick cow. A *love*-sick cow. Why the heck don't you spit it out? Does he beat yer up? Does he give you hell?'

It was a good trick. Worked like a charm. Lorraine leapt to the defence immediately, and Jackie laughed.

'Well, thank God for that,' she said. 'The Invisible Man lives! Honest, Lorraine, you've been giving me the creeps the last long while. What's the big secret? You've got a feller. All right. When I went loonie over Geoff last year I didn't keep you out. What's wrong? Has he got two ruddy heads or summat?'

Lorraine didn't answer right away, just gave a non-committal grunt. The hollow feeling crept back into her stomach and she felt an aching loneliness. Oh Mohammed, Mohammed.

'What fascinates me,' Jackie chattered on, 'is how you've kept it so dark. I mean, I've never seen you with a feller. You never go to none of our places. And where the heck else *is* there in this dump? What d'you *do* all the time?'

'He's got a bike,' said Lorraine. 'A Honda. We go about.'

'Ee, you lucky pig,' said Jackie. 'When do I get to meet him, you tight cow? Scared of the competition, are you? I promise I'll be good.'

She giggled, because she wasn't half as good-looking as Lorraine. But Lorraine wasn't laughing.

'It's not serious,' she muttered. 'I wouldn't care if you did take him. It's been going long enou—'

They were walking along a broad, badly-lit street by the park. Lorraine had to stop because her voice had given up. She started to cry, loudly, leaning against the railings. Jackie put her arms round her and gently pulled her away from the street light. 'Never mind,' she whispered, over and over. 'Never mind, love, never mind.'

It was a long time before Lorraine could speak properly. For ages the only words she could say were, 'You mustn't tell. Anyone. Jackie, it's a secret, you mustn't tell.' By the time she managed to stutter out she was going with a Pakistani, it can't have been much of a shock. Jackie must have seen it coming from a mile off. She went on cooing and hushing till Lorraine was pretty quiet. Then she said: 'Crikey, our kid, what if your old man found out?'

It was a pointless question and they both knew it. Her parents weren't bad, just ordinary folk, but it was impossible. In any case the question Lorraine wanted answering was different altogether. What did Jackie think? Did she hate her for it? How did she respond to the idea of Lorraine and a ... and a black? But she was in love, she couldn't really *listen*. She wanted to talk. They went and sat on a park bench in the warm night and she went on and on, telling Jackie everything. It would have been right monotonous if it'd been just an ordinary fellow, but with him being a Pakistani she could tell there was an edge of fear, a little thrill of horror to keep Jackie fascinated. But she still went on and on, she couldn't help herself. She cracked up Mohammed to be the greatest, the finest, the most fantastic bloke in the world. And one thing – it wasn't because she was desperate, no one could think that. All the fellers were after her, she was always being chatted up. It was her own free choice ...

'Crikey, yeah,' said Jackie. 'You could've had anyone, Lorraine. You could've done far—' She stopped, then said warily: 'Are you, like ... ashamed, love? I mean ... Well ...'

Lorraine would have blown up, but her energy was gone. She considered the question carefully, looked at it from every side, but she didn't dare to actually think. It was a question she wouldn't answer. Couldn't. It was a question that shouldn't be asked.

'You kept it quiet enough,' said Jackie. 'You kept it dark.

Eh up, Lorraine, when I asked you a month ago you said you were going to night school. Laugh! That'd be the day!'

'Well,' said Lorraine, weakly. She looked up at the black sky, studded with stars. Oh Mohammed. Her mind was filed with him, she ached.

'Say nowt, Jackie love, you've got to promise me. It's got to be a secret.' She started to cry, quietly, not a lot. 'Oh Jackie, Jackie,' she said. 'I love him, I love him, I love him.'

On the nights in that summer when the weather wasn't perfect, they found another perfect thing to do. They'd drive the ten or eleven miles down the Oldham Road into Manchester, and go to a cafe in Rusholme, one of the weird and wonderful places there called sweet centres. It was weird and wonderful to Lorraine, anyway, because it was so insanely foreign. Half of the people who ate there were Asians, lots of them in overalls or working clothes, and they had a juke box that played Indian music loudly all the time. The waiter was a jolly, handsome man of about thirty-five who quickly got to know them, and introduced Lorraine to all the sweets of the Orient. Her favourite, which he first called milky sweet, then rasmallai as she got familiar with the names, used to make her shiver with delight, so cool and clean-tasting after a curry. They didn't serve the food with knives and forks – or with rice – and she was shocked for quite a number of times at the idea of picking it up and stuffing it, dripping, into her mouth from a chapati or paratha. She got used to it, though, and became a very neat eater. She never got used to their tea – a cheap glass cup with one third milk and a teabag swizzled round in it for a second or two. And the walls amazed her always. They were panelled, with a tiled picture of an English country scene showing through, advertising Maypole Tea and Maypole Butter. She adored the place.

There were many Pakistanis always in the cafe, and soon they were welcomed as regulars. Mohammed taught her the Moslem greeting and reply, but he always spoke

English, and refused to reply if spoken to in any other language. They were a long way from Oldham, and never thought they would meet anyone they knew there. But when they left one night, not a wet one but a fine, warm, loving night, they walked into an ambush.

The only reason they had gone to the Sweet Centre that night was because they had had such a fantastic day. They had both said they would not be back for their teas and they had set off from the middle of Oldham at not long after five-thirty. They didn't stop after a mile or so to kiss, but Lorraine hugged herself close to Mohammed's narrow, black-leathered back. She had on a thin, flowing dress and a very light wool jacket. Even on the motorbike it wasn't cold. The sun was still high, and beat gently on her shoulders. As she hugged him, she felt a rush of excitement. It was going to be a beautiful time.

Mohammed headed right at Mumps roundabout, then left up the Lees Road. They picked their way through the village, he opened the throttle to climb Lydgate brow, and they dropped at forty-five down through Grasscroft with the exhaust mumbling on the overrun. Right and right again over the railway bridge, a hard left into Greenfield, a jog along to the bottom of the Isle of Skye road, then the long, winding climb up to the high, flat roadway that led across the blasted heather and peat of the moor to Holmfirth. They raced along there, it was derestricted and empty, except for the odd grey suicidal sheep, then took the exhilarating drop down to the town fast and good. At the bottom they turned hard right and began to climb up the back part of the town, up to where they filmed the old TV series called Last of the Summer Wine, up the narrow, difficult, bending road towards the television mast at Holme Moss. Although Lorraine kept her head pressed happily to Mohammed's back, she switched from side to side to watch the various views as they changed. It was wonderful country, with cliffs, woods, water, moors. At last they were cruising down a long long road on one side of a valley that stretched to their right – not fast, the exhaust popping gently inside her helmet. On their left the moor rose a couple of hundred feet to the skyline, behind them a mile was the huge TV mast, and in front of them, at the bottom of the road, hundreds and hundreds of feet lower, a huge reservoir deep in trees. On the right was a small car park, with white railings, an observation point. It was empty except for three daft sheep as they pulled in.

Mohammed switched off the engine, they lifted off their helmets in silence, and in silence they listened. In front of them the valley lay steep and mysterious, its bottom deep in shadow. Neither up nor down the road was there anything moving. Apart from the occasional almost unheard baa of a sheep there was no sound. If there was a breeze it was silent. They climbed off the bike and stood side by side, holding hands, their helmets perched on petrol tank and seat like big red snails. They drew closer together as they watched the lovely stretch of moor and valley. They turned towards each other and clung, arms and lips together.

After a while, still without a word, they strapped the helmets to the bike, turned their backs on the valley, and walked across the road to the rising moor. They had daft shoes on, thin leather and Lorraine with highish heels, but they didn't care. Sometimes the ground was wet, and they had to jump, laughing, from tuft to tuft of the boggy, wiry grass. Sometimes they held hands, often they stopped to gaze and kiss. Then they'd have to scramble, almost on their hands and knees, up steep bits with loose rock. Half-way up Lorraine took off her tights. They were torn, but she didn't like to litter up this lovely spot, so she hid them under a rock, planning to pick them up later, when they came down again. Right at the top of the ridge, she took her shoes off and left them, coloured like a beacon, on a big flat stone.

Standing up there, hand in hand, they looked at their world. Now they could feel the breeze, and it was beautifully cooling on their bodies. Both were panting slightly. Below, the motorbike was a little toy, the white-railed car park like a handkerchief. They could see for miles. Bare bare moors stretching out behind them, the road and the deep valley in front, and higher peaks across the other side. The TV mast stood silent to their right, towering into the sky, with discs and cones pointing out in all directions. Totally alone, in a small barbed-wire compound, probably humming to itself, but they were too far to hear.

They crossed over the ridge, away from the road, and became invisible. Only the curlews that cried above them had them in their view. The curlews and the television mast. Lorraine hardly knew why, but she took her clothes off, slowly, one by one. She stood there naked, the soft wind playing on her warm flesh, her hair curling slowly round her waist and over her right breast. She smiled at Mohammed over the small pile of her clothes. He smiled back, completely relaxed, and started to undress. He too was beautiful, brown and lean, and they lay for ages in the sun, wrapped in each other's arms, listening to the breeze and the curlews, and the sounds of each other's breath and bodies. They lay for ages, with the smell of the warm, sweet grass in their nostrils.

At the Sweet Centre Lorraine had her favourite, meat bhuna, with paratha and a salad. Then she had a double portion of rasmallai. Throughout the meal she sat pressed against Mohammed, and she was glowing inside. It was dark as they turned into the dim little street where the motorbike was parked.

The incident wasn't very violent, but it had an awful effect on them. As they approached the bike, two dark shadows stepped out from behind a van. They were Pakistanis, and Mohammed stiffened. They started to speak to him, brutally, in Urdu. Then the taller one, as quick as a striking snake, stepped up to Lorraine and smacked her face, hard, so that her ears rang and she almost dropped to her knees. He said something, in English, very thickly accented, and she looked at him, dazed. She didn't understand and just stared, slowly shaking her head from side to side. He spoke again, and this time she got some of the words. Dirty trash. Prostitute. Brother. The other man, who was bulky, and shorter than Mohammed, was haranguing him fast and loud, and holding him by the arm. He must have been very strong, because Mohammed was trying to break free, to get at the man who had slapped Lorraine, but he couldn't. There were no more slaps. Both men launched a tirade of shouts against Mohammed, then the taller one pushed him hard in the chest as the bulky one let go his arm. As he staggered backwards they both spat, formally, onto the road and strode off. He looked after them, then came to Lorraine and put his arms around her. They were both shaking.

'Your brothers,' she said. 'Why? Why?'

'They're savages,' he said. 'Monkeys from the trees. Come. Across the road. We'll have to have a drink. I'm sorry he hit you. I'll pay him back for that.'

The Albert, as always, was crowded with Irish and students, and they sat completely private in a corner, enveloped in loud, cheerful conversation. They held hands under the table, sipping their drinks, not talking for a long time. Lorraine's fair skin showed a huge red handmark on the side of her face, which she didn't bother to try and hide.

'How did they know, I wonder,' Lorraine said at last. 'I thought we were safe there. It's miles and miles away.'

'It's a small world,' Mohammed said. 'We've been going there ages now. We should've moved on, mebbe.'

Lorraine thought about that and the thought depressed her.

'Why *should* we?' she muttered. 'We've nowt to be ashamed of.'

After a gap Mohammed said: 'They beat me a couple of weeks ago. I didn't tell you. Not hard, just a warning.

Then they said they'd smash the bike. I said that I'd kill them.'

Lorraine laughed, not with humour.

'Kill them if they touch your bike, nothing if they smack me up. Typical.' She said it without rancour, though. She wasn't blaming him.

'I will do something,' he answered gravely.

'Oh, Mohammed,' she said. 'Can't you leave, love? What's it to do with them? You're nearly twenty. Can't you get a place?' She knew all the answers. He was an apprentice, earned a pittance, even then gave most of it to the family. For the others. The people back home. In Pakistan.

'I scorn them,' he said. 'Try not to fret, love. I scorn them. They're monkeys down from the trees. Don't fret.'

He did not mention her family's attitude, and neither did she. They sipped their drinks almost in silence.

It was almost the end of the long, friendly summer when Lorraine discovered she was pregnant. She sat in the lavatory in Crawthorpe's on the morning she finally gave up kidding herself, with her head in her hands. She didn't cry. She was stunned, dazed. Neither of them had spoken about that sort of thing, she wasn't on the Pill, hadn't the faintest idea how one went about it – and at first when they'd started being lovers she'd got tense and jumpy around when her periods were due in case the worst had happened. But it hadn't, and somehow, inside their love, they'd got to know it just wouldn't. It was nothing to do with them, pregnancy and babies. They were Mohammed and Lorraine. She'd grown so certain, that when Jackie had asked her once if she was – 'you know, all right like that' – Lorraine had said – 'Yes' – so innocently, so unafraid, that Jackie had assumed they didn't make love. Lorraine sat in the lavatory for quite a long time, with thoughts buzzing round her brain almost idly. She'd have to have a test, one of the other girls had done that, it was easy, but she knew, she knew. What would she do? What *did* you do? She shook

113

her head every so often, as if to clear her thoughts. She didn't believe it. It couldn't be true. Not *them*.

Up on the moors above Denshaw, they sat with their backs to a huge rock and talked about it. There was an easterly wind blowing over the Pennines, quite cold, but the westering sun kept them snug against the stone shelter. Lorraine was still more stunned than anything, although when she'd first told Mohammed, as they'd lain in the grass and kissed, she'd had her first real clutch of fear. He had sort of jumped in her arms, given a muscular spasm, and his warm, brown face had slowly drained of blood. When he saw that he'd frightened her he tried to smile, did smile finally, and sat up and placed her back against the rock and comforted her. She could fight the panic, keep the flood at bay, because she was with him, facing more than three hundred mill chimneys on the plain, and the sun was shining. And she still didn't quite believe it. With him it still seemed unreal, untrue. She didn't *feel* pregnant. She couldn't *be* pregnant. Not truly.

But as Mohammed talked, the fear began to creep back. 'What can we *do*?' he kept asking. 'What can we *do*?' And slowly she came to realise that it *was* real, and that neither of them could do anything. He said once: 'But it's easy now? Isn't it? I mean, like, it's legal now, one of them abortion jobs, isn't it?' And she went very cold inside, icy. Because she didn't know, and she knew she didn't know. She knew nothing. No one had ever taught her anything. Mohammed neither, she thought bitterly. And he even had O-levels.

'What about your doctor?' he asked. 'You've got a doctor, haven't you, love?'

The hollow feeling was spreading. She was rapidly becoming empty, vast and empty. She thought of Doctor Whitehead and shuddered. He'd known her since a baby. He'd looked after Mum and Dad for years, since before the war. He'd been there when Frederick was born. She could no more tell Doctor Whitehead she was pregnant than she could fly. Anyway, he'd tell her Mum and Dad, even if he wasn't supposed to. He'd tell them. They'd know.

'There must be someone,' said Mohammed, helplessly. 'There must be someone we could *ask*. There must be someone who'll help us.'

Lorraine leaned her head right back, looking at the high white clouds moving across the blue sky. She'd heard of old crones who did it with knitting needles for fifty quid. I wish I could die, she thought.

'I'll ask Jackie,' she said. 'We'll be all right, love. We'll be all right.' But she didn't feel all right any longer. She felt a deep, blind terror corroding her insides, tearing at her like acid. She could feel it begin to grow, and knew it would go on growing, like a cancer. She was pregnant.

Jackie was a comfort, but not a help. She couldn't take it in at first, just like Lorraine. She treated it like some sort of marvel, like a freak at a fair. She kept saying: 'But love, love, how could you be so *daft*! Don't you know *nothing*, love? How could you be so *daft*!' But when it came down to it, when it came to brass tacks, she didn't know a lot more herself, if anything. She said dead chirpy that she'd sort it out, she'd find addresses and who you went to see, and for a while Lorraine thought she really would, thought it was only a matter of time before something got going. But it didn't. Jackie was as ignorant as she was. No one they knew *knew*. All the other girls who'd got pregnant just got married and that was that. It was all right for posh girls, for students and them that had had an education, but their sort were just in the dark. Lorraine floated along quite helplessly, in limbo once again, feeling the baby growing inside her. And the fear destroying her, eating her, corroding her insides.

One day her mother came into the bedroom while Lorraine was standing naked except for a blouse, looking at her stomach in the dressing-table mirror. Lorraine moved as if to cover herself, or to hide, then just stood there, her arms at her sides, her face still. Her mother sat heavily on the edge of the bed and gave a tired sigh.

'How long's it been, pet? Oh, you poor little love. Why didn't you tell your Mam? Your Dad'll be that upset.'

Upset? That wasn't in it, thought Lorraine sadly. When her Dad found out there'd be ructions. He'd kill her. He'd knock her head off. He'd kick her out into the street. *Then* Mohammed'd have to get a flat, that was something. But she didn't believe it.

'Nearly three months, Mum,' she said. 'I'm sorry. I'm right sorry. It were done for love.'

She went to face her father quite bravely, later that night, when Frederick was in bed. Rain was spattering on the windows and a draught was blowing under the living-room door, lifting the edge of the mat. Her Dad, a heavy-set, stooping man, was sitting nervously in front of the electric fire. It occurred to her that he must have guessed already, since her Mum had obviously told him there was something had to be said.

He was very uncomfortable, kept glancing at her like she was a stranger. She was, in a sense. It was a right long time since she and Dad had last had a cuddle or a kiss. She sat on the edge of a straight-back chair, unconsciously smoothing her dress down over her belly.

'Well,' he said. 'Well, lass.' He coughed, looked hunted. 'No use beating about the bush, like, is there? Who's the feller?' He added as a sort of afterthought: 'You daft young beggar.'

She whispered in a sort of wonder: 'Don't you mind, Dad? I mean ...'

'Course I damnwell mind,' he said brusquely. 'I'm that upset I don't know where to put myself. Of course I damnwell mind, you're me daughter.'

She hung her head.

'I'm sorry, Dad,' she said. 'I'm sorry.'

'Ah,' he said. 'Well.' He drew in a long and noisy breath.

'Who's the feller, lass? Is there to be a wedding? Doris! Come in here!'

Her mother came in meekly from the kitchen. She squeezed Lorraine's arm as she passed, and sat by the table.

'Well,' said her Dad, to no one in particular. 'Here's a fine daughter we've raised up, Doris. Got herself in th'ruddy club.'

'She'll not be the last 'un,' said Mum, placidly. 'Who's the feller, love? Will you marry him?'

'Will he marry her, more like,' said Dad. 'Spoiled goods.'

Neither Lorraine nor her mother said anything to this. It was too dangerous. The mood could change from calm to an explosion in a split-second. Lorraine waited. But the question came again, of course. She couldn't get away from it.

'Who's the feller? Is it anyone we know? I didn't even know you were going with a feller. Get told nowt I don't. In me own rotten house.'

Lorraine bit her lip.

'I can't tell you, Dad,' she said. This was it. She paused, feeling giddy and horribly alone. 'We won't be getting wed.'

She didn't have time to wallow in the realisation that she'd told herself at last the plain unvarnished truth. The mood was changing, turning to the storm. Her father seemed more outraged by her refusal to tell the name than anything else.

'What do you mean "can't tell"?' he said, his normally deep voice rising a fraction. 'What do you mean "can't"? You'll bloody tell me on the instant, lass. "Can't"!'

'George, George,' her mother half muttered. There was silence, everybody breathing fast.

'Daddy,' she said, her voice breaking. 'I can't. Please. I can't.'

His eyes glittered, on the verge of rage, for several

seconds. Then he said: 'Can't means won't and won't'll get you nowt but trouble with me, lass. If you'll not tell me, there's summat wrong, but bugger you, that's all. If you'll not get wed you'll have to get rid, do you hear, the bastard can go down the hospital drain, you dirty little slut. "Can't tell" my arse. You can get rid or get out. You're not having any little bastard under my roof and that's an end to it. Get rid.'

All three of them were shaking, well aware that they were on the edge of a volcano that could blow up in their faces. Outside the wind moaned. Lorraine stood up, her face white and drawn, her eyes huge.

'I'll sort it out, Dad,' she said. 'I'll sort it out. Don't fret, Daddy, I'll sort it out.' She swallowed a sob. 'I'm sorry, Dad,' she said. 'I'm sorry, Mum. I'm sorry.'

She talked to her mother for a long time, later, till two in the morning, with her father snoring in the room next door. She couldn't get rid, she said, she'd made her mind up. The baby was real now, it was a human being. She could not, ever, under any circumstances, get rid.

'But what'll you do, lass?' her mother asked, in anguish. 'He means it, you know, he means it. I expect he wouldn't mind so much except for Frederick, but you know how he is about the little lad. He said to me that if Frederick finds out you're pregnant he'll kill you. He means it, love, he'd do something drastic, I don't know *what* might happen.'

'I'll sort something out, our Mum,' said Lorraine. 'I'll not let Frederick know. I'll sort something out.'

'And *why* can't you tell us who the boy is?' asked her mother. 'Even if he's a married feller or summat we'd get to understand. *Why* can't you tell us, love?'

Lorraine rolled over on the bed and pulled her pink quilt over her face. Her voice was tired, she sounded drained.

'Because I can't, Mum,' she replied. 'Because I can't.'

Sitting in the cafe in the Precinct one evening, the cafe they'd gone to that first night, Lorraine asked Mohammed to do something. Not something specific, but anything. Their hands were touching across the table and anyone who looked close enough, when her coat fell open, could have guessed she was carrying a child. She looked into his dark, troubled eyes, and he looked back, his lip between his teeth.

'I love you, Mohammed,' she said. 'Please. We must do something. I love you.'

There was rain running along the cold empty flagstones of the Precinct, being pushed along by wind. Mohammed's eyes were hunted, and it felt to her as if his hand was cold, as if he didn't care.

'You don't love me any more,' she said, and tears welled up in her eyes. She drew away her hand and pressed it to her face. 'If you love me, you'll have to do something.'

'Lorraine, my darling, my darling. I love you. I do, I love you.'

She waited for the but.

'But *what*, what do you want me to do? What can I do?'

'It'll be showing soon, I'll have to leave home. My Dad'll kick me out if he thinks my little brother could tell.'

'My brothers—' Mohammed began, then broke off. She looked at him fiercely, furious.

'Your brothers *what*?' she demanded. 'Your brothers will kill you if they find out you've got some trash white girl up the stick, is that it? You bastard, Mohammed, you gutless sod.'

He looked at her like a whipped dog. She smiled, surprised by a wave of longing for him, a flood of love.

'They might throw you out, you know! Well they *might*, love. Then we'd both be on the streets. If they knew, if they saw me and knew I were pregnant, they might throw you out! Would they? *Would* they?'

It occurred to Lorraine some nights, when they sat in cafes and the other public places that were the only ones they had to go to now that it was autumn with a vengeance,

119

that if they'd fallen in love at a different time of year, they'd never have been in this mess. If it hadn't been for the moors, and the sunshine, and the dry, they'd never have had anywhere to be lovers! The only private times they got were when the upstairs part of the Sweet Centre had no customers in and the waiter let them sit up there and hold hands and talk. But they didn't go there much, because they didn't know who'd split on them, or when his brothers might turn up again. The only other times they had alone were when Bill had finished early at the workshop, and they'd sit on the back seat of a car being done up, and hug each other in the cold. But he normally worked till well past midnight.

The pressure on Mohammed, she realised, was enormous. She somehow knew it was worse than for her, because she knew he had a way out. They still loved each other, and sometimes she marvelled, almost with joy, at the fact that she was carrying his child, *his* child. Sometimes, for a short while, they were happy. Once, on the moors on a cold, clear, beautiful evening they sat behind a rock and looked at the Oldham lights below them and held each other and cried for half an hour, a strange, disturbing mixture of refound love and loss. As they dropped down Ripponden Road back into the city afterwards, Lorraine felt very grave, as though something majestic and important had happened. They hugged each other when they parted, and kissed lightly, and he left without a word. Better, she sometimes thought, if that had been farewell.

But there were messes to go through. A couple of weeks later when she, desperate, was nagging and nagging in despair that he should find a way for them, save their love, and their lives, and their baby, Mohammed broke under the tension. They were in the park, wrapped in jerseys and coats and still not warm, and he stood bolt upright, almost knocking her over, and let out a sort of howl of pain.

'What can I *do*?' he screamed. 'What can I do? Leave me! Leave me alone! Leave me!'

Then he leaned downwards, his teeth bared, and smacked her face, hard, and stumbled off. She heard the motorbike start up, and its sound slowly fade away, and then return and stop. She looked up unseeing as he came to the bench. All she could think of was the slap. Just like his brother's slap. Just like his brother's.

Two nights later he was not at the spot they'd agreed to meet. She phoned Bill's workshop several times from the coinbox three streets from her house, but he said he had not seen him. The next night, when Mohammed *should* have been at Bill's, the message was the same.

Lorraine left for her Auntie Doreen's near Crewe in a black despair that she knew would never lift. Frederick had remarked three days before that she was getting fat and her father made it very clear that he hadn't changed his mind. She'd packed her cases like a zombie, except for the times she'd gone out to try and get in touch with Mohammed. She'd tried Pritties and she'd tried Bill's. Dozens of times. He'd either disappeared, or everyone was lying for him. She behaved as if she'd gone mad. People along the street watched openly from their windows as she trudged to the coinbox, half a dozen times in an hour. She was sunk in misery and grief.

Once she was there, away in Auntie Doreen's semi on the edge of the softer Cheshire countryside, she gave up all hope of him. He didn't know her new address and there was no way he could discover it. She thought of writing to Jackie, giving it, but she didn't dare in case he never bothered to go to her and try to find it out. She just sent her notice in to Crawthorpe's, she didn't go and visit. She didn't want to meet any of them, to feel their prying or their pity, and she didn't want her job back sometime, anytime, ever. She didn't write to Mohammed care of Pritties for reasons she didn't like to face. She felt abandoned and that was that. There was no point in trying any longer, although she missed him with a bitter ache that never left her, not for a second. It was like she'd been in the office in the spring, waiting and longing, aching to see him. She got awful, vivid memories of him from time to time, smelled the warm grass of the moors as they lay together in the sunshine, felt the weight of his lean and lovely body. She would go and lie down, in a darkened bedroom, on her side to ease her bulging stomach, and stare at the wall for hours on end. Auntie Doreen tried sometimes to cheer her up, but usually made sure everyone left her alone. She was very understanding. Occasionally Mum would visit, and Dad did once, but he wasn't very friendly, try as he might. Frederick only knew she was ill, and had gone away to the country to get better.

One day there was a social worker there, a young, pretty girl called Anne, who smoked a lot and swore a lot, until she saw that it disturbed Lorraine. She talked to Lorraine for hours on end and she understood. She'd had an abortion once, she said, at the end of a long and miserable affair with a man who used to beat her up. It vaguely interested Lorraine to find that social workers were human, too. She wished she'd known Anne before. Before it had been too late, before the mess had overcome them, smashed the wedge between them, made Mohammed run away. They had long chats about the future – Lorraine's future, and the baby's, and the family's. She could never go back home with the baby, that was clear. And what sort of life would she have on her own – and the child? She still loved Mohammed, at times wildly, at times with an edge of bitter hate. Would there be a chance that you and the father would be able to get together if the baby wasn't there? Anne always talked of Mohammed as the father, because she didn't know his name. The ideas that she fed into Lorraine's brain lay there, fermenting over the long, drawn-out, lonely days. Would there be a chance? It was like a slow bombshell in her mind, it gave her a glimpse of glorious, impossible happiness. Her and Mohammed, Mohammed and her. And no lump, no hateful, destructive, disastrous baby. Just the two of them alone, with their motorbike and their moors.

She didn't know when the word adoption was first mentioned, or by whom. She didn't know whether Anne was truly trying to help her or whether it was just a formula, a simple way out invented by society so that there wouldn't be too many poor, crippled people around. She became obsessed with the hope, rather, that it could work. When she was without the lump, when she was free and beautiful once more, she could go back to Mohammed and they would love each other once again, all the good times would come flooding back. This time she'd be on the Pill, Anne would tell her how. She wouldn't care if they couldn't marry, ever. They'd be together. It was enough. It was everything she wanted. One day she agreed.

Nobody rushed her, that was absolute. Anne gave her opportunity after opportunity to change her mind, at times even appeared to be trying to dissuade her. But as the time for her to go to the nursing home drew near, Lorraine got clearer in her mind that it was right. One day Anne brought papers for her to read, and she'd already told her mum and dad. They'd visited, when they'd got her letter, and Dad had been a joy to watch, elated. Mum had been happy as well; happy and sad. But over all, it was obvious. It was right. She could go back home, Frederick would never know, she'd get a job again – Dad bet old Crawthorpe would have her back like a shot – she'd settle down. She sat in a chair half-smiling, not really listening. She was seeing herself with Mohammed once more, was seeing the look on both their faces.

As she and Anne sat alone in the living-room, Anne puffing at a fag, shuffling the papers, it came to Lorraine that still the social worker did not know: no one did. She looked down at her big belly, and wondered how to start. Ah well, it was a little human being now, almost ready to pop out. Someone had to stand up for it.

'He'll be a half-caste, Anne,' she said. 'I want to call him Denny. Short for Dennis.'

Anne smiled easily, totally unshocked, unsurprised.

'Are you sure he'll be a boy, Lorraine?' she asked. 'Some babies turn out girls, you know.'

'He'll be a boy,' said Lorraine. 'I'm going to call him Denny. He'll be a half-caste.'

Anne eyed her levelly.

'Is that why he's had to go?' she asked. 'Is that why the adoption? It's a sod, life, isn't it? It can be. A right sod.' She stopped. 'There'll be about six months before it's final, Lorraine, I told you didn't I? That's not to say you could change your mind easily, because you couldn't. But you're not allowed to sign a thing for nearly two months, then nothing's final for at least another three; you could fight it. There's about six months.'

Lorraine shook her head.

'I can't change my mind,' she said. 'I won't.'

'It's nothing to be ashamed of,' said Anne, looking at her closely. 'That he's black. It doesn't mean you've done wrong, more wrong than if it'd been an ordinary English guy. You must believe me, Lorraine, it's very important. I know it makes things harder, that you get more stick from people, from your mum and dad and that, but you mustn't feel ashamed.'

She thought Anne was going to ask if she'd been right, if Lorraine *did* feel that sense of shame, and she began to panic, in terrible fright as to how she could reply. But Anne just said: 'Do you still love him? The father? You do, don't you, love?'

Lorraine could barely speak.

'Yuh,' she croaked. 'He's not black, he's a Pakistani. He's called Mohammed.' She felt stupid, she knew it was a

124

betrayal. Had Jackie said it was a waste, her going with a Pakistani, or had she dreamed it? She could have done better, she could have had anybody she wanted. Well this was a waste, a terrible, horrible waste, all of it. Her mind was filled with loss and hatred.

In the nursing home south of Crewe, clean and white and pleasant, she held Denny in her arms. Denise, a little girl, not very dark at all, except for her eyes, which were huge and brown and liquid. She did not hold her long, though, because already she could feel an enormous flower of love inside her, growing, ready to burst and engulf her, and she was determined. Denny was fair-skinned, but not that fair-skinned, and her parents must not see her. In any case, she could not stay. The love was Lorraine's, not her mum and dad's, and Dad would chuck her out and keep her chucked. Frederick would never even know this way. Her illness had been cured. Anne said it was best, and Lorraine knew she was right. She held her daughter once, then let her go. They may have stuffed her full of drugs, for all she knew, because she began to feel woozy immediately, her mind began to wander. A sweet little child, a tiny little baby. As she drifted off, it did not seem to have much to do with her. It never had. She tried to think of Mohammed, to think of love. But his face was blurred, and her feelings weren't real, or clear; just woozy. Mohammed, Mohammed, Mohammed, what was it? What was left?

Her eyelids fluttered and she groaned, twisting her head on the deep, white pillow. What had Anne said? Six months before it was final, six months. She groaned once more. She had six months.

My Mate Shofiq
JAN NEEDLE

Since his best friend got himself killed playing chicken on the railway line, Bernard Kershaw has been at a loose end. He's got a gang, including a dead-smart girl called Maureen, but they don't do the sort of exciting things they used to.

His life at home's a mess as well, because his mum is ill in a way he doesn't like to think about. Although he still dreams about being a secret agent, or winning the war single-handed, things aren't really all that good.

Then one morning he sees the quiet Pakistani boy in his class turn into a violent fury to sort out a gang who are stoning some little 'curry kids'. Bernard gets involved, without meaning to at all, and finds himself up against the toughest bullies in the school.

He also finds himself in trouble of a different kind. For Shofiq's family, too, are in a bad way, and the grown-up people who are trying to help them appear to the boys to be set on breaking up everything.

Their attempts to stave off these disasters, and to make some sense of the things they see happening all around them, lead Bernard and Shofiq into confusion and violence.

'It's an angry and powerful novel – but much of it is very funny. The characterization is excellent; the dialogue is vivid. Thoroughly recommended.' *Reviewsheet*

Come To Mecca

FARRUKH DHONDY

This collection of six stories is the winner of the short-story prize in the Collins/Fontana competition for Books for Multi-Ethnic Britain. The stories are all about kids in Britain's cities today – especially Asian and black kids.

There's Jolil, who wanted to learn Kung Fu, and Bonnie and Clyde, who got their names because they were accused of doing the same robbery. There's Esther, whose first Carnival is also a time for growing up, and Lorraine, who confronts authority first at school and later on the streets.

These are real kids, observed with a clarity that is sometimes almost painful, but often very funny. Farrukh Dhondy's observant eye is matched by his ear for language, whether it's taunts in the street, cheek in the classroom, poetry in a West Indian disco or banter and backchat in an Indian café.

'These stories are simply marvellously good, supple and subtle.' *New Society*

Red Shift

ALAN GARNER

They stood in the shelter of the tower, holding each other, rocking with gentleness.

'I love you,' said Jan.

'I'm coming to terms with it.'

'– love you.'

'But there's a gap.'

'Where?'

'I know things, and feel things, but the wrong way round. That's me: all the right answers at none of the right times. I see and can't understand. I need to adjust my spectrum, pull myself away from the blue end. I could do with a red shift. Galaxies and Rectors have them. Why not me?'

Jan wanted no more than to hold him. His words vented. Meaning meant nothing. She wanted him to let the hurt go. He could talk for ever, but not stop holding her. Each second made him less dangerous. And she's not even listening. Why can't I use simple words? They don't stay simple long enough to be spoken. I have not come to terms with her eyes or the smell of her hair.

'A magnificently multi-layered novel . . . and a superbly exciting piece of literature.' *The Times*

The Weirdstone of Brisingamen, The Moon of Gomrath, Elidor, The Owl Service, The Guizer and *The Stone Book Quartet* by Alan Garner are also available in Lions.